ONE GIANT LEAP

Ben Gartner

Praise for *One Giant Leap*

"Ben Gartner is the master of middle-grade voice. I was instantly hooked on this fast-paced space adventure. It's the perfect blend of action, visual storytelling, and mystery."
—Fleur Bradley, author of *Daybreak on Raven Island*

"Space enthusiasts and newcomers alike will appreciate the attention to detail in this meticulously researched adventure story. In turns fascinating, hilarious, and terrifying, you won't be able to put this one down."
—Kerelyn Smith, author of *Mulrox and the Malcognitos*

"*One Giant Leap* is your next great sci-fi read! An authentic narrative voice, a cinematic tone that reels you in, and a perfect mix of action, mystery, and humor."
—Lee Edward Födi, author of *Spell Sweeper*

"Perfect for readers with their head in the stars, this STEM-rich space adventure grounds itself in real science, honest emotions, and the familiar challenges kids face."
—Shawn Peters, author of *The Unforgettable Logan Foster*

"*One Giant Leap* is a thrilling love letter to the past, present, and future of international space exploration, launching readers on a harrowing adventure beyond the Kármán Line fueled by Gartner's signature fast-paced storytelling and meticulously researched details. A worthy middle school homage to *The Right Stuff* and *For All Mankind*."
—Refe Tuma, author of *Frances and the Monster*

"An excellent, STEM-focused narrative that will inspire middle grade readers. With moments of true emotion and self-realization that anchor the story in the complicated realities of adolescence."
—Mary Lanni, reviewer for *School Library Journal*

Also By Ben Gartner

The Eye of Ra series:
The Eye of Ra
Sol Invictus
People of the Sun

Copyright © 2023 Ben Gartner

bengartner.com

Published in the United States of America by Crescent Vista Press. Please direct all inquiries to crescentvistapress.com.

Cover and illustrations by Anne Glenn Design

Library of Congress Control Number: 2022918865

ISBN: 9798987075302 (paperback)
ISBN: 9781734155297 (hardcover)
ISBN: 9798987075319 (ebook)

First Edition, 2023

To my sons, who propel me to great heights.

To the brave adventurers who blast off into space, and to the thousands of people who make that possible.

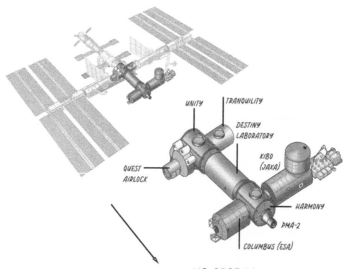

UNITY
TRANQUILITY
DESTINY LABORATORY
KIBO (JAXA)
QUEST AIRLOCK
HARMONY
PMA-2
COLUMBUS (ESA)

US SECTION

INTERNATIONAL SPACE STATION

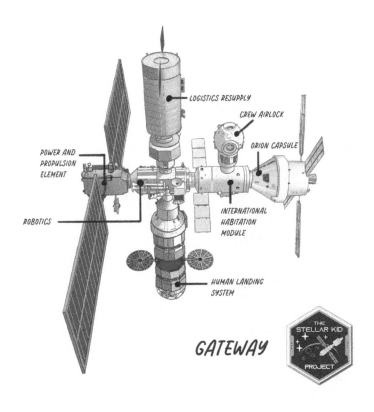

LOGISTICS RESUPPLY

CREW AIRLOCK

POWER AND
PROPULSION
ELEMENT

ORION CAPSULE

ROBOTICS

INTERNATIONAL
HABITATION
MODULE

HUMAN LANDING
SYSTEM

GATEWAY

THE
STELLAR KID
PROJECT

The International Space Station (ISS) travels about 250 miles (400 kilometers) above Earth at 17,500 miles per hour. That is 4.86 miles per second.

The temperature up there fluctuates between 250 degrees Fahrenheit in the sunlight and -250 degrees Fahrenheit in the dark. And because the ISS circles Earth every ninety minutes, the station heats up or cools down every forty-five minutes. That's a lot of wear and tear for a ship that started construction in 1998. It also means that every day, the ISS astronauts get to experience sixteen beautiful sunsets.

The Gateway outpost near the Moon, on the other hand, is about 240,000 miles away. That's almost a thousand times farther than the ISS. Its orbit perpendicular to Earth's means the sun will rarely set on Gateway.

Chapter 1

I'm pretty sure I'm about to die in space. And I just turned twelve and a half.

The frayed end of my tether whips around like a lasso as I flip front over back and sideways.

I see the long blue smear of Earth hurtling past. The silver hull of my ship, the *Aether*, whizzes by in a blur before I gasp at the once-glorious International Space Station. Now, just wreckage. The ISS spits pieces that twinkle in the sunlight. Sparks sizzle and blink against the black backdrop of the endless universe.

My spin continues until all I can see is the void of deep space, punctured by bright pinpricks of gaseous stars millions of light-years away.

The horizon of Earth again, with its clouds and land and water. Home.

The shiny tube of my ship, the *Aether*. It's. So. Close. And yet, it can't save me.

The ISS, Earth, the *Aether*, and here we go again on

this terrible merry-go-round— You get the picture. It's not good. I close my eyes.

I'm tumbling, and I think I'm squirting oxygen from my life-support backpack, which isn't helping my somersaults. My suit is losing pressure. At least that's what I guess is causing the fuzz in my brain. It's hard to think. My vision is narrowing, dimming, like I'm about to wink away.

And the thing that I think is actually going to kill me? Water is leaking from somewhere inside my suit. Quickly it builds up and clings to my face like a wet rag. It's a film over my eyes, it plugs my nose, and it slides into my mouth like alien slime whenever I try to cough. I shake my head violently to jiggle the liquid free, so hard that a nerve cries out in my neck. The head-whip kinda works, and I'm able to suck in a tiny breath. I choke down some water and, though the idea sounds ludicrous, I think, *Am I going to drown . . . in space?*

At this point, you might be asking, "What is a twelve-year-old doing in space?"

And I'd say, "*That's* what you're worried about? Not that I'm going to die?!"

It's cool. Let me answer both questions. Why I'm one of the first kids in space, and how I ended up in this mess, adrift from my craft and about to become a permanent orbiting satellite. If I don't plunge into the atmosphere and burn up first.

I'll pause my death scene to explain a bit about how I got here. Because that's a thing, right? Aren't you curious how I got into this impossible quagmire? It's a pretty amazing story. And 100 percent true.

The books I tend to enjoy reading are about kids being brave, or learning how to be, and I'd like to tell you this is one of those. But I'm not feeling it right now.

To be fair, in those books the kids are fighting fantasy monsters that disappear into dust when you stab them, or they're in a simulation, or a video game, or you kind of know everything's going to be all right, right? It's *fake* danger.

This story is different. This one's real. I honestly don't know how I'm going to survive this. Adrift in space with my oxygen running low, all alone, spinning uncontrollably, a water leak in my suit threatening to drown me.

It all started innocently enough when a harmless package arrived in the mail . . .

Chapter 2

I shall call it the Package of Destiny.

And yes, it came via the regular old postal mail. Not a flying owl. Not an email or a telegram, but that thing in between. Pieces of paper hand carried by a real person to our actual physical mailbox. It always feels special to get a real piece of mail, doesn't it?

I'd built an automated mail-fetching device that would trigger when it detected added weight inside the mailbox. I constructed a slide-out tube of lightweight plastic that sat on top of a finely tuned postal scale inside our box on the street. The mail carrier would insert our letters and junk mail, which would weigh down the scale, which would trigger a servomotor to start, which pulled the tube on a steel cable around a pulley attached to a block of wood right outside our front door. Our porch had a covering so you could shake out your umbrella or stomp off your boots before you came into the house. This is handy if you live in the Pacific Northwest, where it rains a lot. My invention meant that we could get the mail from our box on the curb zip-lined to our door without taking off our slippers. Once you had the deliveries in hand, another button push would send the container whirring in reverse along its cable until it nestled itself back into place inside the mailbox on the street. Pretty simple piece of engineering, really.

That day's mail was special. Not like "birthday money in the mail" special. No, this was no check for twelve dollars from Great-Aunt Mary (she sends me the amount of my age). Nope, this was something far greater. Life-changing, I can safely say. Maybe even life-ending, but I didn't know that then.

A plain manilla envelope that, once I opened it, I'd never be able to go back to "before opening the Package of Destiny" again. I brought it inside and laid it on the little table in our kitchen. I stared at it.

I wanted to hold on to this anticipation and not spoil the thrill of the *possibility* that I could be accepted. I waited hours, keeping myself busy with other things, enjoying this feeling of potential, taking side-glances at it every time I walked through the kitchen.

The sun set. No one was home, as usual, lately.

I was standing in the dim light, just staring at the Package of Destiny, still not sure if I really wanted to open it and learn my fate. I didn't want to read words of rejection, because then the hope would end.

It practically glowed as I read my name for the hundredth time:

> Finley Ridley Scott
> 327 Ganymede Circle
> Gossamer, WA 98099

My stomach did a flippity-flop, and not because it still felt weird to see my name next to our new address. For the other hundredth time, I read the return address in the upper-left corner:

> Axis Space
> 1 Dream Loop
> Estrellas, CA 93400

I was surprised they'd sent it snail mail. I mean, the application and submission had been online, and this was a cutting-edge space travel and tourism company that had sent people around the Moon. But I was glad they did, because it was exciting to hold a physical packet in my hand.

Finally I succumbed to curiosity and ripped it open. A few stickers fell out. And bookmarks in the shape of the Minotaur Heavy booster! And a very cool patch for the StellarKid Project, which showed tiny little versions of the ISS, the Gateway outpost, the Moon, and four stars representing the four winners.

As awesome as the swag was, I ignored it and the brochures and went straight to the letter. It was addressed to "Mr. Scott." Glad to see they got my name right. Since my last name is more like a first name and my first name is more like a last name, I answer to Scott too. But people who know me call me Fin.

Dear Mr. Scott,

As you know, the StellarKid Project received tens of thousands of applications from children ages ten to fifteen from all over the world. Reviewing the submissions and making a decision to invite only four of those deserving applicants was an immensely difficult challenge.

However, at Axis Space, we relish a good challenge. And it is clear that you do too.

Your submission of the SAFER (Simplified Aid for EVA Rescue) was analyzed by—

Oh, come on already! I really wanted to skim and get to the verdict, but also savor every word. And part of me feared the answer would not be what I needed, so why rush to the doom?

If I didn't get accepted, that would be okay, I lied to myself. That's what I expected anyway, not to be a Chosen One, so it wasn't as if it'd be a big surprise. I'd never won anything before, and this would be like a truckload of winning lottery tickets.

All this swag and the colorful brochures and the hand-signed letter is awesome enough, right? I tried to convince myself, but I couldn't. Working on the SAFER had been fun and felt like a win on its own. I mean, the thing would save lives.

But who was I kidding? I really hoped this contest would be my ticket out of here. Not only would I get the once-in-a-lifetime dream trip of flying into outer space and around the Moon, but it would also be about as far away from my problems at home as I could possibly get.

Enough, Fin, just keep reading!

Your submission of the SAFER (Simplified Aid for EVA Rescue) was analyzed by a team of top-notch rocket scientists and mission planners, and was deemed a revolutionary lifesaving tool that we plan to add to our standard equipment. We would like to test it in microgravity, which is where you come in.

On behalf of the sponsor of this trip, Toyohiro, we are honored to invite you to the Axis and NASA training facilities in Houston, Texas, in preparation for your trip into space aboard our flagship Aether spacecraft. If you accept, you and a guardian will visit the International Space Station before your three-day trip to the Gateway outpost orbiting the Moon. From there, you will coast near the lunar surface before returning to Earth. During your journey, in the safety of the spacious Aether spacecraft, you will test a prototype SAFER unit manufactured by Axis and NASA engineers, based on your initial design.

This weeklong journey and all training for you and your guardian will be fully paid for by Toyohiro, the artist-

scientist benefactor who has already so generously donated much of his fortune to schools and libraries around the world.

If you accept this all-expenses-paid adventure, please have your parent or legal guardian sign the enclosed contracts and return them to Axis Space within 72 hours of receipt. We are eager to begin your training.

You are a magnificent young person and we thank you for your scientific contribution to humanity. Your voyage will advance spaceflight and help drive our passion for exploration.

The mission of Axis Space is to make space travel readily available to everyone. Thank you for helping us achieve that dream.

Sincerely,

Jennifer Gabardon, PhD

CEO, Axis Space

And a handwritten note below: *Can't wait to meet you, Fin!*

I could barely breathe. I staggered and plopped into a chair at the little round table in our kitchen, choked out a breath, and read the letter again while chills coursed over every inch of my skin.

This was not what I'd been expecting.

It must be a joke. Who would do this to me?

I turned the paper over. Nothing on the back. I examined the letterhead. The Axis logo looked so real, the white swoosh of the *A* with a red arc through it like a rocket headed to space. The forger had done a miraculous likeness.

I checked the envelope again, peeled the sticker, bent the patch. Someone had gone to great lengths to fool me.

I laughed at myself. It must be real. Right? It had to be. I knew it was.

I leaned back in my chair. This kitchen looked different, like I was in an alternate version of my own life, the fading sunset light coming in through the window over the sink brighter than it had been just a moment ago, "before" I'd opened the Package of Destiny and read the letter. The world had changed.

Am I going to space?

I stared at the letter.

I had a golden ticket. This priceless piece of paper glowed before my eyes.

I shivered and exhaled, staring at the empty signature line on the contract.

RELEASE OF LIABILITY

Oh, that didn't sound good.

To make it all come true, I had to tell my parents. And that would be difficult.

Chapter 3

You see, both my parents were at the hospital. Not like "at the hospital for a quick minute," but more like "basically living at the hospital." Well, Dad came home to shower and get fresh clothes, but Mom was still recovering from her work accident, in which she'd almost died. Dad was by her side as often as he could be. I had gone a few times, but I didn't like it there. I don't want to talk about that right now.

And I hadn't exactly told them about my secret entry into the StellarKid Project contest.

Uncle Dennis would check on me when my dad stayed late with Mom, or I'd head over to his house. Uncle Dennis lives three streets over on Callisto Street.

With the Package of Destiny in my backpack, I jumped on my old clunker bike, which was too small for me, and pedaled like a circus bear over to my funcle's house. I call him that because he's my fun uncle, my funcle. He's let me drive his car a few times in the empty mall parking lot. But don't tell my mom that. She wouldn't have approved of me driving yet, or of me biking in the dark. Lucky that she wasn't there to stop me. Oof, poor choice of words. Her accident was anything but lucky.

"Uncle D?" I announced myself as I entered through the back door.

"In here," he said from the living room. "Grab yourself a soda. I'll take a root beer." Nighttime soda is also something my parents would disapprove of, but gotta love the funcle.

I grabbed two and went into the darkened room, the glare of the television strobing on my uncle's face. He was watching a survival reality show called *Alone in Alaska.*

"These clowns don't know what they're doing. I could totally win the million bucks," he said, cracking open the root beer. Uncle Dennis had been an Air Force pilot for a bunch of years but was grounded because of something to do with his vision. He hadn't loved that change of pace, and his growing gut reflected the slowed-down lifestyle.

"I need to talk to you, Uncle D." I set the Package of Destiny on the coffee table on top of some old *National Geographic* and *Aviator Life* magazines.

"Oh?" He looked over at me. He knew I didn't usually say that sort of thing.

I nodded, biting my lip.

The TV winked off, and he stood to turn on a lamp.

"You had dinner yet?"

"No. Not hungry."

That was also something I didn't say very often.

"Fin, you all right? What's up?"

"The Package of Destiny." I nodded toward it on the table. "It's gonna change everything for me."

"The Package of Destiny." He said it with a dramatic flourish and a clenched fist. "What is it?" Uncle Dennis sat back down. The couch wheezed dust satellites into the air around us.

"You've heard of the Artemis program?"

"The NASA program, sure. Everyone's heard of it. Put the first woman, first person of color, and the next man on the Moon since the last boots left in 1972. Amazing, isn't it?" He took a slug from his root beer. "What about it?"

"And you've heard of Toyohiro?"

Uncle Dennis frowned and scrubbed at his scraggly beard. "Think so. Rich dude, right? He's like two hundred years old or something?" He grinned.

I chuckled. "Something like that. So, have you heard of the StellarKid Project?"

"I have . . ." he singsonged, leading me to go on.

"I entered."

"You did? That's awesome."

"And I won."

Uncle Dennis spit root beer through his nose. "Ow! That burns."

I laughed.

He wiped his face with his shirt. "Wait, really? You won?"

"Well, I'm one of four kid winners."

"Fin!" He stood and threw his arms wide, spilling more root beer onto the carpet. "Really?! That's amazing!" He bent over, set the soda down, and put his big hands on my shoulders. He stared at me with his eyes as wide as they would go. "Fin. Really? You're not pulling my leg?"

"Well, I think so. Read this." I opened the Package of Destiny and handed him the letter signed by Dr. Jennifer Gabardon, the leader and public face of Axis. The woman you can find all over the Internet and who I'd studied for years. I idolized her, still do. She doesn't care what anyone thinks. She'd make wild, outlandish claims about the future or her company's goals, people would scoff, and then she'd make it happen anyway. With her leadership, Axis was regularly ferrying people and supplies to the ISS and to the Gateway outpost, as well as to another new station, the Genesis, being constructed for space tourism in low Earth orbit by a private company.

Uncle Dennis sped through the letter, tracing the

words with his finger. He scrubbed at his beard, shot
glances at me, and read the letter yet again.

"Fin, wow. Wow." He fell back onto the couch,
shaking his head. More dust particles launched into the
atmosphere. "This is very, very cool. I'm speechless.
And jealous."

"There's one problem." I sighed.

"What?" He turned his head to me and paused.
Realization hit. "Oh."

Then a second later, with our eyes locked, he added,
"Ooooh."

"Yeah."

He held up the letter, tracing his finger again until he
found the snippet for which he was searching. "'This
weeklong journey and all training for you and your
guardian,' it says, Fin. 'Your guardian.' It doesn't say it
has to be a parent. I mean, obviously your mom can't
go, and I'm sure your dad would love to, but—"

"There's no way he would leave Mom right now."

"No way." Uncle Dennis shook his head firmly in
agreement. "And you? Are you okay to leave your
mom right now?"

"There's nothing I can do."

"Well, maybe not." He looked away. "This is an
amazing opportunity, Fin. I think your mom will want
you to go."

I waited until he took a drink from his root beer.

Now.

"I want you to go with me, Uncle D."

Perfect timing. More root beer shot from his nose.

"Ow! Quit doing that to me. It hurts!"

I laughed. "Totally got you."

"Wait, are you joking?"

"I want you to go to space with me." I snorted. "Don't hear that every day."

"No, you certainly don't."

"The catch, though," I said, letting it hang for a moment, "is that you have to help me get Mom and Dad to sign the forms. You have to talk to them with me."

Uncle Dennis lowered his eyes. "I see. I get it now. Okay."

He itched at his chin. "Fin, I'm honored. I mean, it's a no-brainer that you'd choose me, but still, I'm flattered." He smirked. "And of course I want to go with you, Fin. But talking to your parents is something *you* need to do. I can't do that for you."

"I don't want to," I snapped, and stood. "I want to get out of here, Uncle D. Far away from all this mess, my mom in the hospital, me basically living alone. But I can't tell *them* that. Come on."

"I wonder if you want something else," he said, one finger on the dimple in his chin.

"I want to go to space, of course."

"Mm-hmm." He nodded slowly, examining me.

"What?"

"The hardest part is being honest with yourself. Trust me, I know this." He rolled his eyes. "And once you figure that out, the next-hardest part is telling someone you can trust with those things."

He stared at me, expecting something. I had no idea what.

I shrugged.

"It can take time, but think about what you *really* want. You say you want to get out of here, that you don't even want to talk to your parents about this awesome thing you did, but there just might be something else going on."

"Funcle, come on."

"Think about it. That's all I'm saying." He threw his palms up in defense. "And if you ever want to talk, I'm here for you. You know that, right?"

"Actually, there is something."

"Okay." He settled into the couch cushion and put on an "I'm serious and listening" face.

"Honestly?"

"Of course."

"I honestly want pizza right now."

A smile arced across his lips and he pulled me in for a hug. "I love you, my little Fin-kabob."

"I know, Uncle D."

He stood, pulled his phone out of his pocket, and told it to call Pizza Planet, our favorite pie place. "That's right, Jimmy. The usual. Pineapple, pepperoni, green peppers, and black olives."

He hung up.

"Tomorrow," I said. "Visiting hours. You're coming with me."

"Sure," he said. "I'll even put on pants."

"Wow, you really want to go to space."

"You could say I have high hopes."

Oh man, poor Uncle D, such a groaner. But I loved it.

I laughed, but I had a pit in my stomach that wasn't hunger. It was from thinking about seeing my mom tomorrow. I loved my mom, but I hated that place.

Chapter 4

Who loves the hospital? That's right, no one. It smells funny, and the lighting is weird, and there are very few people smiling. I didn't even like to make eye contact or breathe in the germs. Of course, I loved my mom enough to push through that stuff. But I still hated to go. I hated seeing her in bed with tubes attached and reliant on other people if she had to pee. It was depressing and freaky.

Uncle D was with me, so at least that helped.

"She just fell asleep after physical therapy," Dad said in the hallway outside her room. I peered in through the little rectangular window, and a breath caught in my chest. She looked dead, pale and frozen in time. Then I saw her eye twitch, and I released my breath. I wanted so badly to hug her right then.

I pushed open the door and ran to her and threw my arms around her. She stank of B.O. and old sheets.

"Fin—" My dad half-heartedly tried to stop me.

I didn't want to cry, so I didn't. And even though she needed a shower, it was still my mom's stink.

She didn't wake up. I looked at my dad. He'd followed me in. "Is she okay?"

Uncle Dennis ran his hand over my mom's head of blond hair.

My dad adjusted his glasses and then scratched his eyebrow. Oh, geez, if he was tearing up, then I'd tear up. Please don't.

"Guess what, Dad?" I whispered. I tried to sound upbeat while I changed the subject. I had to be strong for my dad.

Dad smiled, and I saw his Adam's apple bob up and down. "What, kiddo?" He stepped back toward the door and gestured for me to follow.

When we were back outside the room with the door ajar, I handed him the Package of Destiny. "I need you and Mom to sign this."

He gave me an inquisitive look with a raised eyebrow.

"It's a pretty big deal, and I know now is not a great time with Mom and all, but it's only for a few months, and I really, really want to go, and Uncle Dennis said he'd go with me and—"

"Whoa, slow down." He put his hand on my shoulder.

"I haven't agreed to anything," Uncle Dennis said,

shooting me a glance. "Yet."

I felt slightly betrayed by his comment, but I guess it was technically true.

"Where do you want to go?" My dad opened the envelope and pulled out the letter, which I would definitely frame later. "Axis Space? StellarKid Project? Toyohiro?" He kept reading as if everything was a question.

"I won, Dad. I won. I'm going to space."

He snorted. "Space?"

"For free." I flipped to the dreaded piece of paper labeled RELEASE OF LIABILITY. "I just need you to sign this and then I can go to space. They need an answer quick, Dad, so—" I held out a pen.

"Fin, wow. You won." He ran a hand through his hair, then laughed and pulled me in tight for a hug. "You are amazing, Fin. I'm so proud of you."

I didn't say a word, just enjoyed the moment.

Then he released me and looked again at the contract. "This is a lot to digest." He looked back through the window at my mom sleeping. "I'm so proud of you, but I need to discuss it with your mother. I mean, sending you to space is not something that . . . I don't know, Fin. It doesn't seem like the right time, with your mother the way—"

"Now's exactly the right time!" I snapped. "I'm practically living alone or with Uncle Dennis anyway.

What does it matter if I'm up in space or sitting in the dark at home?"

My dad huffed through his nose, and his shoulders slumped. He closed the contract and inserted it quietly back into its envelope. My hopes were waning like a dimming moon.

"Uncle D will be with me, Dad," I pleaded.

"Hold on, Fin. I haven't agreed to anything yet," my supposed funcle said again.

"Come on, Uncle D, what the heck?!"

"I don't know, Fin," my dad repeated.

Were they ganging up on me?

This was ridiculous. A trip to space! What was there to know?!

The agitation rose up through my belly. My chest tightened, and I clenched my jaw. "God! You never let me do anything! We moved to this stupid town away from my friends and then Mom had her accident—"

I choked. I couldn't finish the sentence.

"Fin, calm down," Dad said, gesturing to Mom's door.

I shouted. I knew I shouldn't have, but I couldn't stop it. I didn't want to. "No! I will not be calm! I am going whether you like it or not!"

As soon as I said it, I knew it was silly. But I was just so mad.

My dad wrapped his arms around me. He wasn't a

whole lot taller than me, but he was a lot bigger around, and stronger.

He hugged me tight.

"Leave me alone!" I screamed. "God, I hate you!"

A nurse down the hall turned to look.

Dad let go of me. "Fin."

I spun around, fear and anger engorging my face, my hands shaking. I could hear my heart in my ears.

Over his shoulder, I saw Mom, awake, frowning, the saddest look creasing the skin above her eyes.

"Fin, we'll look it over, okay?" my dad said, waving the Package of Destiny.

"Whatever." I spun on my heel and stormed away.

What a punk, right? I know. I'm embarrassed about it, but I know we've all been there. When you're so mad and frustrated, it makes your brain boil. It's like the dark side takes control.

That night, after I'd had a chance to cool down, I texted my dad.

Home for dinner? Uncle D is making pasta and I'm making the salad.

Just a second later I saw the three dots, indicating he was typing back. Then they disappeared. I waited. Nothing.

"Fine," I huffed. I guess I had my answer.

"No dice?" Uncle D asked, dumping the marinara

out of the jar and into a pan.

Ding. I had a text.

It was from Mom. My throat tightened.

We'd talked just yesterday and still I missed her.

I unlocked my phone and read her text.

Congratulations, Fin. You are AMAZING. We signed the contract, and your dad will bring it home with him at dinner. I love you. I'm proud of you. Can't wait to talk more about it. Tomorrow, okay?

What? Just like that? They signed?

So, wait, that meant that I was really going. I was really going to space.

Wait for it—annnnnnd it finished sinking in.

"Woo-hoo!" I shouted, and jumped in our little kitchen. I wrapped my arms around Uncle D's back.

"Oh, that can only mean one thing," Uncle D said, putting down the wooden spoon and turning to face me.

"I'm going to the Moon, Uncle D!"

"Wait a second," he said, suddenly looking stern. "I think you mean *we're* going to the Moon." His face broke into a huge open-mouthed guffaw, and he threw his arms in the air.

"Ha ha ha!" I jumped again and hugged him tight. "Oh man, this is—this is—"

I slumped down into a chair.

It was unreal.

And as it settled in, I felt . . . *guilty*. For what I'd screamed at my dad. For making my mom sad.

But they were okay. Right? Mom understood. I'd give my dad a hug tonight and apologize. It'd be fiiiiine.

I was going to space. I was really going to space.

And finally getting out of there.

Chapter 5

My recurring nightmare starts out awesome. I'm the pilot of an F/A-18 Navy fighter jet, rip-roaring through the atmosphere at Mach 1, the speed of sound, almost 800 miles per hour. I tip my wings and can feel the extra vibration shudder through the frame. It's an extreme feeling of power, and I love it, but then my jet jumps, and I know something is wrong even before the alarm starts blaring and the red lights start flashing.

The computer tells me one of my turbofan engines is on fire.

I'm losing altitude. The impact with the earth will kill me, but I'll explode before that if the fire hits my fuel.

EJECT EJECT EJECT flashes on my heads-up display. I'm frozen. I stare at the HUD.

The jet jerks violently to the side, and I'm thrown against my harness. My helmet smashes into the canopy. I see stars.

EJECT EJECT EJECT

I know it's going to hurt if I do it, if I abandon my aircraft. I'm terrified. But there are no good options here, and I know what I have to do.

I yank on the ejection handle, and the canopy explodes up and away. My eardrums burst. The wind howls. A bomb detonates underneath me and shoots me up and out like a bullet. The launch whips my head forward, my chin crushing into my chest, cranking my neck too hard, much too hard. The pain is incredible. My body compresses with unbearable g-forces, I can't breathe, my vision blurs, and . . .

That's when I wake in a cold sweat.

I try to wiggle my toes, but I can't move them. Sleep paralysis. It usually goes away after a few seconds, but when I wake with that immediate sense of impending doom, and I can't move, it's petrifying.

Chapter 6

In a matter of days, the other winners and I went from just a bunch of random kids to "The Kids Going to Space!" Along with me, there was Mae Jorgenson from South Africa, who wore a dark leather jacket, flew crop dusters on her parents' farm, and served as our resident expert on space junk; David Kalkutten from Norway, who had won a gold medal in the Olympics and was all about two things: athletics and video games; and Kalpana Agarwal from India, who, though she was extremely humble and shy, was rumored to have learned to code before she spoke her first words.

After Axis and NASA announced our names and broadcast our faces, we became overnight global celebrities. I didn't hate it, but I certainly didn't love it. After we did the final press interview before heading off to training, we went into a media blackout. I was relieved. So was Shelley Mitchell, the public relations coordinator who'd tried to guide our every word, which had been like teaching cats to dance. Managing a bunch of kids was not her forte.

Training, on the other hand, was super fun. Not as fun as the launch, but I was challenged. And I love learning, so I couldn't get enough of it. I mean, I've been really into space ever since I was in fourth grade and NASA launched a new rover to Mars. I made a whole website about the planets and the satellites. My teacher showcased it in front of my whole class. I knew all about the original Moon mission and drew the stages of the *Saturn V* rocket, along with the full flight plan of Apollo 11 through the lunar landing and reentry to Earth, and hung it on my bedroom wall. I made models of rockets from scratch and of my own design using 3D CAD software, and launched them in the park on calm days. I even engineered a new parachute assembly for the model rockets, for which I submitted a patent application. It's pending review.

A detailed model of the ISS hangs over my bed, floating 250 miles below the real thing. Mom put up some glow-in-the-dark stars on my bedroom walls, accurate down to the constellations visible from the Northern Hemisphere. For my next birthday, I wanted a more powerful telescope.

Anyway, I think you get my point. I'm definitely a space junkie.

That reminds me of a story: One winter night, on

vacation in Colorado and out sledding with my parents after dinner, my dad caught me looking up at the Moon. He put his arm around my shoulders and told me, in all sincerity, that someday I would go up there. I looked over at him with a knowing grin and a gleam in my eye, believing it to be obvious, like Dad had finally figured out what I already knew. That's the moment when we *both* knew it would happen.

You could say training was a little like summer camp, except instead of canoeing and eating s'mores, we were training for our lives in the simulators. Six days a week for three months, working and living with my crewmates. And yes, we had some regular playtime too. Turns out I'm not bad at volleyball.

Another reason it was like summer camp is that we only mixed with our guardians mostly at dinner or on the weekends. There were a few times when one of the parents came to watch their kid, but our daytime training was typically separate from the adults' track. I was okay with this, just like school. And it was fun to swap stories with Uncle D at night, just like after coming home from school.

I called my mom and dad and filled them in on all the events, though I felt a little guilty talking about how much fun I was having. Like, because they couldn't be there. And also like I should have felt bad to be away from them. I mean, I missed them, but I was having a blast. Plus, I'm not really a phone guy. So the calls were usually pretty brief.

It went by in a flash too. Three months of training might sound like a lot, but that is of course waaaaay less than real astronauts. Real astronauts have to learn everything about living and working in space, *plus* they train for their particular mission, whether it be a scientific endeavor or replacing a busted radiator array. And, of course, they're trained on how to fix the toilet and replace the carbon dioxide scrubbers and all the other necessary maintenance. Astronauts work All. The. Time.

They play, too, because there has to be time to rest. But mostly, they work, work, work, trying to take advantage of their time off-Earth.

Besides the labs and the simulators, we also spent a lot of time in the classroom, listening to a PhD elaborate on orbital mechanics or how to pee in space. It's the coolest classroom in the universe and some of your teachers are literally rocket scientists.

Chapter 7

I first met Commander Marc Horowitz, the man in charge of our *Aether* spacecraft, when he came to monitor an exercise we were doing with our space suits.

This was the first time I'd put my hands on the prototype SAFER that NASA and Axis built for our trip. I had mocked up a few different designs using spare parts in my shed at home, but those didn't compare with seeing the real thing. It was awesome. Basically, it was just a rectangular block that attached to the bottom of the life-support system on the suit's back, but with arms that extended up either side of the pack and also around to the front. Tiny holes in the arms would spurt compressed nitrogen to let you navigate in three dimensions—pitch, yaw, and roll.

"It's a beauty," Commander Horowitz said, snapping the SAFER into place on our test suit.

He was a slim guy with a square jaw covered in

stubble and kind of reminded me of my math teacher. But unlike my math teacher, who gets very animated explaining division of fractions, the commander is extremely calm. All of the time. Always. I'd never seen him get excited about anything. I think you could drop him into the middle of a tornado and he'd be perfectly capable of serving high tea. I've never been to high tea, but it sounds delicate and not something easily done in a tornado. Unless you're Commander Marc Horowitz.

The training session on that day was about how quickly we could get in and out of our EMU—the extravehicular mobility unit, aka the space suit—if there was an emergency. Like, say, a depressurization in the cabin caused by a puncture to the hull. The tech explaining the drill, Jason, was a thin, red-haired, freckly guy who didn't look much older than my co-winner David Kalkutten. David was a pretty big guy, though.

"Okay, we're going to time how fast you can work as a team to get one person in, and then out, of your space suit. As you can see"—he laid a hand gently on the shoulder of the EMU, hanging on its mount—"these are sort of gangly contraptions."

Gangly was how I'd describe Jason, not necessarily the EMU. The space suit is more like a miniature spacecraft with full life-support systems (even if you have to pee in a diaper). It's made of multiple complex pieces of machinery and can withstand the harsh environment and extreme temperatures of the vacuum of space. Does that sound like a "gangly contraption"?

"And getting it on is very difficult without some help," Jason continued. "We'll walk you through it a few times, and then we'll let you go for it as a team, each person taking a turn being the one who gets suited up. If you can't make it in under the target time, you fail the test."

They'd been trying to scare us with the F word a lot. *Failure.* If we failed these tests, we could still lose the mission and not get to go. Our trip wasn't guaranteed. The media beforehand had sure made it seem like we were going to step off the stage and into the rocket, but we had a lot of hard work to do. And we kept being reminded that we could wash out at any stage. That was also why the commander was there. He really wanted to see us succeed.

And be safe. If we got hurt and if it was bad enough, we couldn't go. If we failed the classroom tests or the emergency-preparedness drills, we would put not only ourselves in danger, but the whole crew, the whole mission, and thus we'd be benched.

"I'm going to be the fastest," Mae said.

"What do you mean?" I sneered. "This is a team time. There's no winner here."

"Sure, Moon boy." She blew a fake kiss. She'd started

calling me "Moon boy" after she learned of the crescent moon birthmark at my hairline. The adults thought it was simply a reference to our trip to the Moon, and I didn't feel like tattling on her. I patted my hair down to cover it up. I don't know why I hid it. Just felt like an imperfection, I guess.

"We'll be fast," David said, stepping in between Mae and me. "Ladies first." He gave a little bow to Mae, gesturing to the EMU with one hand, the other on his stomach.

"No, that's okay. You can go first, David," she said. I thought it funny she completely overlooked the other girl in our group. Kal, which is what we called her now, didn't react at all, which didn't surprise me.

David acknowledged Kal, though.

"Oh, you go ahead," she said, shaking her head. The streak of purple in her dark hair flashed.

David shrugged to me and put his fist out. "For who goes first?"

We'd invented a new version of rock-paper-scissors called asteroid-moon-planet. Planet beats moon, moon beats asteroid, and asteroid beats planet (as the dinosaurs could tell you!).

I smirked. "You think you can beat me now for some reason?"

He made a face. "Best of three."

I put my fist on my palm, and we pumped together.

"Asteroid. Moon. Planet."

On the third pump, we both held our fingers out flat in the symbol of an asteroid (like a pancake, which is what you'd be if you got hit by one). Tie.

Tried again. This time, I shaped my hand into a crescent moon. David held out his fingers flat again for asteroid. Moon beats asteroid because Earth's moon provides some protection from asteroids. I won that round. 1–0.

In the next battle, David chose planet, keeping his hand in a fist. But I knew he was going to do that, so I chose asteroid and wrapped my fingers around his fist, indicating triumph. 2–0. Clean sweep.

"Fine. You're up," David said, pushing a loose strand of hair behind his ear.

Jason had his stopwatch ready to go. When that timer started, I jumped into the bulky pants, then wriggled and wrangled my way into the main torso component suspended on a mounted bracket. The girls attached the glove units, and David simultaneously brought down the helmet. But the gloves hitched and didn't snap into place right away. And David went very slow with the helmet. I think he was worried about hurting me by clipping an ear or something.

Once everything was locked in place, David patted my helmet and stepped back and spoke in his native Norwegian. "Ferdig!"

Jason made a big show of stopping the timer, then gave an impressed look at the watch. "Well done, my little cadets." *Little cadets?* "You beat the target already. Barely, but you did it."

A man in a dark suit with a pencil-thin tie and a mustache to match walked over and patted the top of my helmet as if I were his pet. When he scowled at me, a thick, pale scar on his chin showed itself. "Not bad, *kids.* Now let's see if you can do that under the stress of a real disaster." He snorted and waved his hand dismissively. "Put 'em in the NBL and see how they do." The man literally rolled his eyes, which seemed childish and uncalled for. What was his deal?

I got the distinct impression that this guy thought we were a joke.

"Uh, for real, Mr. Deuce, sir?" Jason asked. "The recovery test in the Neutral Buoyancy Lab is usually for experienced astronauts only."

The NBL was the humongous pool that housed a life-size replica of portions of the ISS, where astronauts trained for their space-walk missions.

Mr. Deuce shot Jason a wicked stare. Then he turned it into a fake smile that reminded me of a Disney villain, with the protruding cheekbones to match. "Of course not. They'd fail, and this mission wouldn't get off the ground. It'd all be over so soon." I didn't know this guy, but based on the higher pitch of how he said it, it sure sounded like he was being sarcastic.

So he was expecting us to fail? Or he wanted us to?

Guess we'd have to show him how wrong he was about us.

He turned and walked away, right into Commander Horowitz, who didn't budge. "Do you have something to say, Alfred?"

The man stepped back, out of the sphere of Commander Horowitz. "Commander."

"Accountant." The commander said it like a slight.

"Yes," Mr. Deuce said, swiveling his head around at all of us. "Yes, I do have something that needs to be said. What you're doing here is dangerous and foolish, and it prevents us from doing *real* work." He tugged at his crisp suit coat and straightened his tie.

"And you don't think that being a part of this historic mission to take the first children—our best and brightest—into space is 'real work'?" The commander put his fists on his hips. It made for an imposing presence despite his average stature.

"You don't intimidate me, Horowitz. Guys like you come and go, and guys like me are the ones who decide it. Out of my way."

"You're a paper pusher. These kids are the real heroes." He pointed at us.

"Well, we'll see about that. I'm not the only one who thinks you're wasting time and money."

"Sad to see you go, Deuce." The commander turned to the side and let the man pass.

We were silent.

Then the commander spoke to us, but loud enough that Mr. Deuce would probably hear as he strode briskly away. "Don't worry about him. That man only has numbers between his ears, especially number two."

I stifled a laugh and saw Mr. Deuce falter in his steps.

Once the double doors closed behind the accountant, Commander Horowitz clapped his hands and rubbed them together. "Now, that first run was good. But let's see what you can really do."

I agreed. That first run was kinda sloppy. We could do better. "Again!"

"We already beat the target," Mae said. "Let's just finish the rest of us so we can move on."

"I wanna drill again," I said. "Is that okay, Jason?"

"You're being irrational." Mae crossed her arms. "I wanna get to something more interesting, like the flight simulators. It's not like any of the rest of us are going to get to don a suit in space."

Mae was referencing my planned test run of the SAFER prototype inside the *Aether* hull while en route to the Moon. I was the only one who would get that honor.

"It's okay," David said, mostly to Mae. "We go again?"

Mae huffed. "Fine."

David understood. This was a competition with ourselves, as a team. To do better, to *be* better. We could be the best.

Eventually, I'm happy to say, we actually set the record.

I do like to win.

Chapter 8

The next time I saw Mr. Deuce, we passed him in the hall on our way to the centrifuge training area. He wore the same black suit, black tie, and starched white shirt. No one said anything as we crossed paths, but when I looked at him, he flashed a tiny little smug smirk.

I *really* wanted to prove that guy wrong.

The door opened as we approached, and standing there was a man wearing a blue flight suit with the NASA logo patch on his breast pocket. He was about as tall as me, but stockier, tanner, maybe Italian or something. He had neatly trimmed black facial hair, with no gaps in it like Uncle Dennis's. I think I'd look good in a nice, solid beard like that.

"Who's ready for some g-forces?" he announced, excitedly.

Commander Horowitz introduced us. "Cadets, this is Mission Specialist Glenn Barrera."

"Howdy, kids." Specialist Barrera gave a curt wave.

"Glenn's specialty is botany," Commander Horowitz continued. "He's researching a plant's ability to reproduce and grow in artificial gravity. His latest design is a big spinning doughnut."

"Ha. It's much healthier than a doughnut. All leafy greens growing inside the ring, each sticking toward the center as the doughnut spins around to simulate gravity." He gestured with his hands. "It's up on the Gateway right now, and I can't wait to visit."

"Could your design scale to human size?" Kal asked.

Specialist Barrera looked impressed. "Potentially. That is one potential application, yes. On a grander scale, for humans on long cosmic voyages, it could help with things like bone-density loss if we had a way to simulate gravity, like the centrifuge you're going to ride in a few minutes. But for now, my studies are still relegated to the more near-term needs: food and the nutrients that fresh greens provide. Though they do also serve as carbon dioxide scrubbers. But primarily, fresh food. If you've been in space for two months, there's nothing as priceless as a bite of a tomato or a leaf of real butterhead lettuce. Mm, mmm."

My mind was still stuck on the "long cosmic voyages." Imagine traveling deep into space for years at a time. Maybe my grandkids will get to do that.

"Okay, that's enough. Let's not get Glenn too excited,

or he may wet his plants," Commander Horowitz joked, grasping Specialist Barrera by the shoulder. "As you know, NASA is sending us with two hitchhikers for a drop-off on Gateway, which is orbiting the Moon. Mission Specialist Barrera is one of them. And you'll meet Dr. Sally Sokolov when we run through the software sims in a few days."

"Okay, so, who's ready for some extra g?" Specialist Barrera backed up through the doorway, revealing the control room to the centrifuge. A woman with a badge hanging around her neck that read *Marta* sat at the panel of dials and switches. I expected it to be more computerized, but sometimes dials and switches will do the job.

The bulky steel arm of the centrifuge held a capsule at its end, counterbalanced by a weight on the other end. Buoyed at its center of gravity by a girder cemented securely into the floor and through the ceiling, the centrifuge spins its occupant around in circles like the Tilt-A-Whirl or the Gravitron at the mid-state fair, Specialist Barrera told us.

"Except, where those carnival rides might hit two or maybe three g," Commander Horowitz explained, "this baby can simulate up to twenty g. That's twenty times the force of terrestrial gravity here on Earth, way more than what your body is normally used to, and actually more than it can endure for any prolonged period. When you have all those g's pushing the blood away from your brain, your color vision goes, then your vision tunnels, and then you're effectively blind, but still awake." He had his hands up to his head like horse blinders. "Then you black out completely. Your brain can't function without the blood, and you lose consciousness. But as soon as those g's are reduced, you recover fine as long as it's done in time. Disoriented, yes, but physically unharmed."

"Sounds like you've experienced it," Mae said.

"I have." He nodded thoughtfully. I thought there was a story there, but he wasn't divulging more.

"What is the max g you've ever experienced?" I asked.

Specialist Barrera chuckled. "Well, I passed out around nine g, but I'm sure the commander here could sustain that while banking in his jet."

Commander Horowitz nodded, a serious look on his face. "That's true. But we train extensively in centrifuges similar to this, and we wear a G suit that compresses our lower legs to help circulate the blood."

"So, he cheats," Specialist Barrera joked.

"Can you die from it?" Kal asked, cutting the humor.

"It's possible. Fifteen g's for a minute, for example, can be deadly to humans. But we're not going to get anywhere near that today."

"Or during launch," Commander Horowitz added.

"We might spike around four g's, but even that would be temporary. For liftoff and reentry, we'll experience a sustained three g."

"Ah, I was hoping for more," Mae, the pilot, said.

"No more than a carnival ride, boo."

"Something like that. The vibrations are a different story, but, yeah, liftoff is fun." Commander Horowitz smiled.

And I'd get to do it! If I didn't wash out first. So far, so good, but I must admit I was a little nervous about the centrifuge. I heard that it brought out the worst in some people. As in, it made them puke.

"So, who wants to go first?" Specialist Barrera asked.

"I went first on the suit training, so someone else can go first here," I said.

"I want to go first on the flight sim," Mae said.

"You can go, David." Kal seemed a little nervous about the idea too.

"Yeah, show us how it's done, David. You're used to extra g-forces on the gymnast rings, or whatever they're called, right?" I said.

"No problem," he said, grinning.

Turned out, there was a problem.

"Okay, we're going to start you up real slow now," the tech, Marta, said over the intercom.

From the control room, we could see the centrifuge

through a window and David close-up on a monitor, strapped into the capsule. Next to the view of him was another screen displaying his vital signs, like heart rate and blood pressure.

Marta slid a lever and watched a dial move up to 1.5x.

"You are at one-and-a-half times the force of gravity now, David. How are you feeling?" she asked.

"No problem," he answered, flashing us a thumbs-up.

"Okay, great. Moving to two g."

Through the window, we could see the metal arm moving in a circle, but it didn't look very fast. And the monitor view of David in the seat didn't hint at any kind of movement. It was just David sitting there like he was waiting for takeoff.

"See? No big deal," I said to Kal, quietly.

She smiled at me but didn't respond immediately. When she spoke, she said, "It's not the speed. It's the confined space."

She was claustrophobic? "Ah." I paused. Wait. "But you'll be okay on the *Aether* for a week?"

"Have you seen the inside of the *Aether*?"

"True. It's very spacious. I think you could fit my apartment in there." I hated my new apartment. "Downsizing," my dad called it.

"Bigger than an airplane, and I'm fine on those."

"Well, good. Think you can get through this exercise?" I didn't want her to wash out.

"I will. Thank you for asking." She smiled.

"Course. We're a team." I shrugged. "Hey, you hear about the claustrophobic astronaut?"

"No?"

"He just needed a little space."

Kal snorted through her nose and put her hand to her mouth, like she didn't want me to see her teeth, while shaking her head at me.

"Sir," Marta said over her shoulder, "I think we may have a problem."

The dial indicating g-forces steadily rose, inching past three and on its way up.

"What's wrong, Marta?" Commander Horowitz stepped forward and leaned down.

Marta whispered something in his ear. He straightened back up, brow furrowed in thought, looking at the controls. "Try again."

She put her hand on the little black lever, and that's when I noticed it was all the way down, to the off position. Out the window, the centrifuge still spun. On the monitor, David was grinning, obviously enjoying the ride. The dial crept past four g.

Marta pushed the lever up, then down again, but nothing changed.

Five g.

David was blinking his eyes rapidly, the smile gone. "Uh, guys? Time to stop?" His voice was strained, the vessels in his neck bulging as if he was working hard not to fall over.

"Abort the run," Commander Horowitz directed. "Immediately."

Six g.

Marta slapped the big red emergency button.

Seven g. David's eyes lolled back in their sockets and his head flopped to the side, unconscious but still pinned to the headrest by the g-forces.

Commander Horowitz smashed his fist down on the emergency abort button, mashing it several times.

Eight g.

"Oh my god," Mae said, a hand over her mouth. "Help him!"

"Cut the power!" Marta exclaimed, pointing to a big red arm on the side of a circuit-breaker box behind me.

I rushed over and yanked it down.

Instantly, we were plunged into darkness.

Commander Horowitz flipped on a flashlight and shined it through the window into the centrifuge. The capsule was slowing, quickly. It came to a smooth stop, and we rushed in to see if David was okay.

Marta opened the hatch, and a wave of rank sour smell hit our nostrils.

Commander Horowitz aimed the light at David,

sitting there, squinting at the light in his eyes, with vomit down the front of his shirt.

"Did I fail?" he said.

I laughed in relief. We all did.

"No, son, you didn't fail. You passed with flying colors," Commander Horowitz said. "You got up to seven g's before passing out. That's amazing."

David gave a weak smile. "But I threw up."

"We'll get you cleaned up." Marta helped unbuckle and pull him out. He walked away on wobbly legs, leaning on Marta and Mae.

"I had a very real dream," David said. Then, his eyes down and more to himself, "Of Mom."

"Vivid dreams can be associated with G-LOC," Marta said. "That's g-force-induced loss of consciousness."

I know it wasn't the same, but I thought of that recurring nightmare of mine. The ejection from the cockpit and the tremendous g-forces.

Then I thought of David's mom. We'd never talked about her, just like we hadn't talked about mine. But the media wrote about us, so I knew David's mom was in prison in Norway and had been ever since David was a toddler. The blogs had written about my mom too, but I didn't read them.

David's dad was the one who was going to blast off into space with us.

David was about the exact opposite of his dad, who was overweight with short, thinning brown hair he combed over from one side. And, also unlike David, Chris Kalkutten knew basically zero about space. He was a nice guy, but he made cheese for a living and didn't seem to like physical activity much. I truly wondered if David was adopted.

For example, when David introduced us and he said I could call him Chris, I said, "Oh, like Chris Hadfield. Have you seen his video of 'Space Oddity' on the ISS?"

Of course, we'd all seen it.

But Chris looked at me like I'd just spoken in Russian. He didn't know Chris Hadfield?! Sheesh, Commander Hadfield's guitar-floating rendition of that Bowie song got about four jillion likes online. It's a classic. Besides the other videos he made in space, which were awesome too.

Maybe lucky for Kal and her claustrophobia, NASA shut down the 20-G Centrifuge for investigation into what happened with David. I was bummed I didn't get to try it, but Commander Horowitz told us we weren't off the hook. They had another unit that was smaller, that you lie down on, to give us some preparedness for launch. The Short Radius Centrifuge was open to the room, so no enclosed capsule.

Kal did fine. She didn't even puke.

Chapter 9

"Easy does it," *Aether's* pilot, Captain Eileen Gurkin, informed Mae, who was now at the controls of our simulation spacecraft. A French woman, the captain spoke English as well as, or better than, most of the Americans I knew. She was one of those people who smiled easily and had rosy cheeks. The lines around her eyes proved that she smiled a lot over her entire life, not just for us.

"Doucement," she said, patting her hand in the air. I interpreted this as a reiteration of "Easy does it."

In the window, the ISS docking port was getting closer.

"All you need is a tiny burst of the propellant to adjust your attitude," she instructed. "I can tell you've flown a plane, but you can't fly the *Aether* like that. No, the vacuum of space is different. There is no gravity or friction to slow you down. Remember that every action has an equal and opposite reaction. A little shot of compressed air to get us spinning and we'd never stop unless you counteract it with another spritz in the opposite direction."

Mae nodded, listening intently. I'd never seen her so rapt. She was in heaven. She'd told us that her other mom, not the one with us on this trip, let her fly their little two-seater on their farm in South Africa.

"The twelve thruster quads will control your pitch, yaw, and roll," Captain Gurkin continued. "The combination of those measurements, along with your delta-vee, which you can think of as your speed—"

"The change in velocity," Mae said. "Delta-vee."

"Yes. Since we're already traveling 27,000 kilometers per hour without any additional thrust, we talk instead about delta-vee, or the changes we're making, when initiating a burn. Or, as in this case, maneuvering for a very delicate docking insertion."

Mae nodded like she knew all of this already. As our resident space-junk expert, she'd wowed us with some wild statistics about how much human-made trash is floating around up there. And how even a tiny piece of debris could cause a massive problem for satellites, or spacecraft, or even the ISS. She compared it to the enormous Pacific Ocean plastic garbage patch floating around, except the bits in space were flying fast enough to kill an astronaut in an instant.

"And the combination of pitch, yaw, roll, and delta-vee measurements equals what? You were about to say?" Kal asked.

"Those define our orientation relative to the other objects around us, what we call our attitude," Captain Gurkin finished.

"I think Mae's attitude is fine," David said, flashing the thumbs-up.

Give me a break, I thought. David and Mae kept flirting with each other more and more. It was getting sort of groan-worthy, actually.

"Kal, systems status," Commander Horowitz said.

"Altitude 401 kilometers," Kal read from the display in front of her. "Life-support systems look good."

"Life-support systems *nominal*," Commander Horowitz corrected. "Another space-ism. Does anyone know why we don't just say *normal*?"

"Because *nominal* doesn't mean 'normal.' It means 'as planned.'" I knew that one.

"That's right. Nothing about space travel is 'normal.' For example, the booster oxygen level might be at 95 percent sitting on the launchpad and that would be 'nominal,' as planned. But mere seconds after liftoff, after we've burned hundreds of gallons of propellant to get that beautiful beast off the pad, we'd be at a much lower percentage, which, at that later time, might also be reported as 'nominal.'"

"Next time my dad asks how I think I did on my

math test, I'll tell him 'nominal' and see how that goes," I joked.

"Careful," Captain Gurkin said to Mae. She pointed at a screen of numbers. "You're a bit off course on the trajectory."

"Copy," Mae said. She gave one of the joysticks a gentle tap, and I felt the delta-vee of movement to the side.

But the push didn't stop when Mae let up from the control. We could still hear and feel the propellant shooting from its thruster.

"That's not right," Mae said. She tapped the other direction, and the opposite thruster fired, trying to balance us out. But when she let go again, the opposite thruster didn't quit either. Now we had two opposite thrusters spurting propellant out into space, fighting each other for control of our spin. The *Aether* started to shimmy and shake, strained from the battle of the opposing forces.

A red light started flashing repeatedly.

"Warning. Warning. Collision with ISS at current trajectory. Engage autopilot?" a vaguely British person asked, the voice of the onboard computer.

"Captain Gurkin?" Commander Horowitz leaned forward in his chair to look over at our pilot.

"It's okay," she said. "Computer, engage autopilot. Abort docking."

"Warning. Warning. Collision with ISS at current trajectory in ten seconds."

The autopilot hadn't engaged. Mae looked to Captain Gurkin, frantic, her hands an inch from the joystick, like she wanted to take back control but didn't know how to save us.

"Everyone, visors down, seal your suits," Commander Horowitz ordered, in that calm, casual way of his.

Captain Gurkin jammed on the thrusters, trying to reverse our direction. Out the front windows, we could see the PMA-2 docking port on the ISS approaching, much faster than we wanted, and our ship was wobbling. We'd crash into the station with the spear-like tip of our docking mechanism, potentially puncturing the vessel. And if we lost pressure in our cabin too . . .

"Se presser! Hurry!" Captain Gurkin exclaimed, motioning for me to close my visor and seal my suit in case of cabin-pressure loss.

It all happened so quickly.

As I moved my arm up to my helmet, the *Aether* slammed into the ISS. Our lights went dark, and everything stopped. I could hear my own heavy breathing inside my suit.

No one spoke. We all knew what had happened.

"Well, we're all dead," Mae said, letting the controls

snap back into their default position.

The lights came on.

Horowitz flipped up his visor, unbuckled, and stood. "Wait here. We'll run it again in a minute. Get some water, if you need it."

He walked over to the hatch and opened it, stepping out onto the runway that led to the control station for the spacecraft simulator.

I heard his terse tone. "What was that? I didn't order any curveballs for Mae's first flight in the sim!"

"I don't know, sir," Jason, the tech, replied. "We're running diagnostics now."

"Oh, too bad," someone said. I recognized that creepy voice. Deuce. "Guess we'll have to mark that down as a failure."

"Did you do this?" Commander Horowitz snapped. His normally calm voice now had an edge to it.

"Commander," Deuce replied, "I'm shocked you would insinuate malfeasance. I am merely observing the progress of our young cadets after what happened in the centrifuge."

Silence. I couldn't see what was happening, but I imagined an intense stare-off, with laser beams shooting from their eyes and meeting halfway in a shower of sparks. Green from Horowitz and red from Deuce.

"Jason, I don't want this paper pusher anywhere

near the controls. Got it?"

"Uh, yes, sir," Jason said. I chuckled at the guy caught in the middle of the turf war. But I guess the commander outranked the accountant.

"Run it again," the commander said, his voice getting nearer to us. Then I heard his footsteps on the metal grate of the platform that led to the *Aether* simulator. We were still buckled into our harnesses, waiting as instructed.

Commander Horowitz closed the hatch and buckled himself back in. "From the top, Captain Gurkin. But let's have Mae fly it from the beginning."

"Really?" Mae said, obviously excited.

"You were doing great until that glitch. I want to see you nail that docking."

"And we could run through how to avoid that type of disaster," Captain Gurkin added. "Whether intentional or not, that was a good reminder that accidents can and do happen in space. They happen in a flash, and training for worst-case scenarios is something we do constantly here at NASA."

"Plan for the worst, hope for the best," Kal said. "Kinda like my asteroid-hunting software."

"Mae, honey." It was Mae's stepmom on the radio. "Sorry to interrupt, sweetie, but I wanted you to know you're doing an A-plus job and I'm very proud of you. Be careful, okay?"

I think we were all surprised to hear her voice. I felt embarrassed for Mae, but not as much as Mae felt, I'm sure. Mae rolled her eyes *hard* at almost everything from her stepmom's mouth, which is pretty rude, maybe. But I get it.

Peggy Jorgenson, one of Mae's moms (not the pilot one), was always bubbly, and she wore pastel pinks and baby blues.

Maybe that's why Mae likes the black-leather-jacket attire.

Mae didn't talk about her situation at home, or her moms, at all. I guess we had that in common.

On the next run of the sim, Mae crushed it. She was a natural.

David, being the gamer, did pretty good too.

Kal was too timid on the controls. She said she preferred the navigator role, being in charge of the computer's logistics.

As for me, I did okay. But, as you'll hear later, piloting wasn't my best skill.

Chapter 10

"The analysis came back from Kalpana's StellarKid Project software. Asteroid L289-A has an 88.4 percent chance of intersecting with Earth orbit in four years."

Dr. Sally Sokolov, a Ukrainian, the other mission specialist we were dropping off at Gateway, delivered this dire news, pointing at a grainy dot on a large monitor in front of the classroom. "Your mission is to calculate the force and mass necessary to deflect or divert it from its current course."

"And save Earth!" I shouted, my finger thrust into the air.

Dr. Sokolov grinned. Her face had soft lines, almost like she was slightly out of focus. Her voice was soothing even when delivering Earth-destroying news. I'm guessing this had to do with her bedside manner, since she was a physician. A surgeon, actually. Thus, Dr. Sokolov was our crew's medical officer. A role we hoped we'd never need.

Plan for the worst, hope for the best, right?

"Where will you begin your calculations, Kalpana?" Rakesh said. Kal's dad had asked to sit in on this exercise.

Kal seemed to shrink a little with the question, but she answered promptly. "The vector of most likely convergence, Baba."

"No," he replied with a bit of forced patience, "you'll first double-check manually that the software has identified a true threat."

To me, it seemed like Kal had kinda said that, maybe?

"Of course, Baba." She bowed a little but didn't meet his eye.

From what I'd seen of the two of them, it was pretty much always like that. Kal had won an International Academic Decathlon! You'd think her dad would, by default, be proud of her. But he always moved the goalpost when she succeeded. It was hard to watch. I mean, he seemed like a nice enough guy, and I'm sure he was acting with good intentions, but just say "good job" and leave it at that, right?!

My parents, on the other hand, were almost annoyingly supportive. My presence here was evidence of that. My mom was in the hospital, my dad was taking care of her all by himself, plus taking care of me—and I'd yelled at him for it.

"That's okay, beti. Learn from your mistakes and move on."

Mistake? What mistake?

"David and I will double-check the math, Kal. You can work on the vector," I butted in.

"No, I'll do it," she responded quickly. "Thank you, though."

"Okay," David said. "We'll work on how to divert, Fin."

"We'll work on how to divert Fin? That sounds good," Mae said, shooting me a glance like a challenge.

"You know why Darth Vader loves the Moon?" I asked.

"Why?" David played along.

"Like Mae, it has a dark side."

"Oh!" David laughed and bit his knuckle, looking at Mae for her reaction. She punched him in the arm, a real slug. David rubbed his shoulder and laughed some more.

I turned around to my computer and noticed that Kal was completely ignoring us, her head down and working the problem. Her dad hovered nearby.

I wondered if that was why Kal didn't say much. Less chance of being judged. Maybe she was bottling those feelings inside. With that pressure building, I hoped she didn't pop one of these days like a Mentos dropped in soda.

That could be dangerous on a flight to the Moon, trapped in a small space for a week together, with literally no outlet.

Kal had just finished delivering her results to the group when Mr. Deuce strolled in.

"What are you doing here, Deuce?" Commander Horowitz asked.

"I saw the results of Kalpana's software and must admit, I was impressed," he said, supposedly genuine. "I wanted to come by and congratulate the young cadet myself."

He walked up to Kal and offered his hand. She looked to her father, who nodded once. Then she looked to Commander Horowitz, who raised an eyebrow and shrugged.

"Thank you, sir," she said, and took Mr. Deuce's hand.

"You've done admirably well, for a child," he said. "I'm sure you'll have a place at NASA in a few years, when you're ready. Until then, this exercise was completely staged, you realize. I suppose we should all be happy that your software didn't actually find any asteroids on an intersect course with Earth. The problem is, your software didn't find any asteroids at all. None. And we know there are plenty of them out there circling between Mars and Jupiter in the asteroid belt. Odd, wouldn't you say?"

I am not a violent person by nature, but man, I wanted to punch that guy in his thin, crooked nose.

"Get out of here, Deuce. Enough," Commander Horowitz said. "Don't you have better things to do than pick on kids?"

"I'm sorry, sir, you must be mistaken," Mr. Agarwal said. "My daughter's software works impeccably."

"Of course it does," Commander Horowitz said. "Don't let this guy get under your skin, Rakesh. He's just lonely."

"With David's illness in the centrifuge, Mae's disastrous destruction of the ISS in the sim, and Kalpana's disappointing software, I'm afraid we'll have to bump the trip," Mr. Deuce said. "Perhaps we can reevaluate during the next opportunity. The schedule might open up in 2030 or so."

That was years away!

"I've already filed the termination papers," Mr. Deuce said.

"Oh, Deuce, you're not stopping this mission. Ultimate go/no-go decision falls to the administrator, and to me. From what I've seen, this crew is ready."

My chest inflated at hearing the commander talk about us like that.

"There's no way Administrator Gould will let you sabotage it," the commander said, crossing his arms.

"We'll see, Commander. We'll see." Mr. Deuce turned on his heel and walked away, leaving us a little dumbstruck.

"What do we do?" Mae asked.

"Nothing. Deuce thinks he's a big man, but he's just a scared little boy trying to push others around because he thinks it makes him important."

"But can he stop our mission?" Kal asked.

"No." Commander Horowitz responded so quickly, and with a smile, that I couldn't help but believe him.

So why was I scared he was wrong?

Chapter 11

"Hi, Dad," I said into Uncle D's phone. "How's it going?"

"Fine, fine," my dad said. "How was your day?"

I hadn't told him about the centrifuge accident, and I didn't want to tell him about Deuce and all that either. "Good."

"Good. High and low?" he asked.

We did this with school too. You'd name one highlight of your day and one low point. Some people call this game "rose and thorn."

"High was . . ." I thought about it. I didn't know. "Well, I thought it might be talking to Mom. Is she there? Are you at the hospital?"

"She came home yesterday, Fin. They finished construction on the new accommodations for Mom, so we're home now."

"Oh, that's great!" I said, but I caught myself thinking how glad I was not to be home with them.

What a terrible thought, I know! But there it was. I didn't know what to say next. "Well, there's my high. That you are home now."

"Yeah, she's—she's pretty tired right now, Fin. I'm sorry." Dad wasn't telling me something.

"When I talked to her last night, she seemed fine. Is she okay?"

"Yeah, just tired. Long day. The adjustment of leaving the hospital has taken a lot of . . . energy." Then he brightened up. I could tell he was forcing it. "But she's a champion and doing great. Persistent, you know your mother."

I chuckled for my dad. Then there was a too-long pause between us. "Tomorrow we hear our go/no-go decision from NASA about whether we're deemed ready to fly."

"Oh boy, you nervous?"

"Nah, we got this," I said. I thought about Mr. Deuce and whether we really would get to launch.

"So, any low?" he asked.

"Um." I hesitated. "Nope," I lied. "Woulda been nice to talk to Mom. Tell her hi for me."

"Proud of you, Fin."

"Yep."

"Okay, then. You must be tired too. Get some good rest for your big day tomorrow. Tell your uncle hi for me, okay?"

I heard a moan in the background, then a scratching sound like he had put the phone to his shirt. I could tell he was speaking, but not to me.

I waited a second. "Dad?"

"Fin, I love you. Mom says she loves you too and she'll talk to you tomorrow."

"K."

The phone went dead and I stood there for a few seconds, frustrated.

I couldn't wait to blast off.

Chapter 12

When the administrator herself, Dr. Josette Gould, met with us the next day in a conference room at Johnson Space Center, I was visibly nervous. I didn't think I would be, until we got there, and I fully realized that it came down to this one meeting. Probably the most important and pivotal moment in my life so far, where this woman would decide our fate. We'd soon know if we were going to space or not.

The ultimate go/no-go. I told myself my shaking was from excitement. That was a trick I'd learned from a teacher, to try to convert the nervous energy into positive excitement.

Dr. Gould had wide shoulders and bushy red eyebrows. She wore a blue-and-white suit with an American flag pin on the lapel.

"Josette, how are you?" Commander Horowitz said. It seemed awfully informal, given the weight of this meeting. "How's Eric?"

Who's Eric?

"He's good. Adjusting to an empty nest since Joan moved to Harvard. Thanks for asking, Marc." Dr. Gould shook the commander's hand and grabbed him at the elbow in a friendly embrace. Commander Horowitz was wearing a short-sleeved polo shirt with the Axis Space logo on it, and I saw the muscles in his forearm flex. "You still hittin' 'em straight over at muni?"

"Most of the time. But, darn it, 90 percent of the putts I hit short don't go in," Commander Horowitz said.

Dr. Gould chuckled.

I had no idea what they were talking about.

"Golf," Uncle D whispered. He must have seen my confused expression.

"Dr. Gould, I'd like you to meet the rest of my crew." Commander Horowitz introduced the *Aether* flight crew first—Pilot Eileen Gurkin, Mission Specialist Glenn Barrera, and Mission Specialist Sally Sokolov. Handshakes all around.

"And, Josette, these are the amazing students who won the StellarKid Project—Kal, Mae, David, and Fin. And their guardians Rakesh Agarwal, Peggy Jorgenson, Chris Kalkutten, and Dennis Scott."

Dr. Gould shook our hands, then our guardians'. "Congratulations to each of you. To have made it this far—wow. You should be immensely proud of what you've accomplished. Your projects are truly outstanding." She gestured to the conference room. "Please, let's sit."

When we'd settled in, I wondered who would speak first.

Dr. Gould leaned forward and put both elbows on the table. "It's a shame what Marta found."

Commander Horowitz nodded solemnly, a stern expression pulling his lips tight, as if holding back some angry, vile words.

"In all my years, I've never experienced anyone tampering with the equipment at JSC," he finally said.

Kal startled and squirmed in her seat.

"We are under constant threat," Dr. Gould said. "From enemies foreign and domestic who would be happy to see us fail in our mission, Marc. You know that."

"But I've never seen it. It's unprecedented. And a shame to be targeting these innocent kids."

"Marta found concrete evidence that someone disabled the safety mechanisms in the centrifuge. That is a felony offense. Without the quick thinking to shut down the power . . ."

She implied a potential grisly consequence for David. I remembered Specialist Barrera explaining that fifteen g's for a minute would be fatal. When we saved

David's life, we assumed it was a malfunction, not a deliberate attempt.

"Do you know who did it?" Uncle D asked.

I remembered the sly look on Mr. Deuce's face as we crossed paths in the hall on the way to the centrifuge control room. Or when Commander Horowitz challenged him in the simulator control room. Should I say something?

"Not yet. We're looking for evidence and making a case. Unfortunately, I can't comment on an active investigation," Dr. Gould said. "But, needless to say, there are a lot of eyes on this mission. More than just the usual space geeks—this one has a lot of political attention. And people above my pay grade are pressuring me to make a decision about this endeavor. It goes all the way to the top."

"That's why we're here, Josette," Commander Horowitz said, looking at us. "I know this is your decision, but I wanted you to meet the brave men, women, and children who have trained for this launch."

"You are all, indeed, the cream of the crop. The world will know your names forever," Dr. Gould said. "But you must understand. If something goes sideways, and, god forbid, someone is—*hurt* on this mission, it could be detrimental for the entire space program, risking young lives like this. There are parties who think the exploration of space is money wasted, resources that could be better utilized for research and development here on Earth, not off-planet. If someone is already trying to sabotage this mission, and were they to succeed, it would be a very public failure and would invite tremendous criticism. I'm not being overly dramatic here when I say that it could shut us down. No more Moon missions. Gateway ceases development. No Mars, Commander."

"Understood," Commander Horowitz said. "But we can't let them win. You know this in your heart. If we give up now, they've won. These young people have captivated the world with *possibility*. With *potential*. Josette, they are the embodiment of *hope*. Of what we as a global species are capable of when we come together."

Dr. Gould chuckled and looked down at the table for a moment. Then she looked around the room at us again. "Heck of a speech, Marc. It's no wonder they made you the commander. It certainly wasn't because of your golf game."

"Flying a rocket 250,000 miles into space is a lot easier," Commander Horowitz said. "These kids deserve a shot at space, Dr. Gould. What do you say?"

The NASA administrator stood and paced, her hand squeezing the back of her neck. "Are you certain, Commander, that these kids can handle it? That these *civilians* can handle it?"

"These aren't the first civilians in space, Josette."

"The first that could be my grandkids, though."

"They can do it." Commander Horowitz didn't flinch.

"Are you certain, Commander, that *you* can handle the heavy responsibility of making sure they come home in one piece, no matter the cost?" Dr. Gould leaned her hands onto the table and stared stoically into Commander Horowitz's face.

"No matter the cost, ma'am." Our commander held the stare.

Dr. Gould straightened and put out her hand. "Looks like you've got yourself a go, Commander. Congratulations."

Chapter 13

After the go decision, things moved fast. The next day, we flew on an Axis jet to Kennedy Space Center in Florida. As we circled KSC, Commander Horowitz pointed out the *Aether* on launchpad 39A, the same pad from which *Saturn V* had first carried the Apollo astronauts to the Moon, the same pad from which the Space Launch System had more recently carried the Artemis missions back to the Moon. A legendary and historic site, needless to say.

Before Artemis III, the last human to set foot on the lunar surface was Eugene Cernan in 1972 during the Apollo 17 mission. Before leaving, Mr. Cernan traced his kid's initials in the moondust. That's probably still up there. I wonder if his great-grandkids will visit it someday.

The Artemis program had been busy. And companies like Axis were an important part of NASA's plan for the Artemis missions, since the *Aether* also ferried crew and supplies into space for NASA.

By the way, I think it's supercool NASA named the program Artemis, since the Greek goddess Artemis was the twin sister of the Greek god Apollo. Apollo put the first man on the Moon. Artemis put the first woman. Those NASA scientists, they're pretty smart.

Two days later, on launch day, we put on our flight suits like it was another training exercise. Then we drove to the launchpad 39A, where we got a very up-close view of the *Aether* sitting high atop the Minotaur Heavy booster. Almost 400 feet tall, the giant silver tube sparkled in the sun. Steam and water vapor frothed from the engineering miracle taking us to space in a few hours.

Kal pushed her finger under my chin to close my gaping mouth.

What can I say? I was in awe.

The *Aether* can take off and land vertically. The first astronauts were shot into space in a capsule that sat on top of a bunch of different stages of rockets that got discarded after launch. The *Saturn V* rocket that launched Armstrong, Collins, and Aldrin to the Moon on Apollo 11 was 363 feet tall, but the command module—the capsule at the tippy top in which they returned—was only 12 feet of that. Made of aluminum, like a soda can. Though, to be accurate, the heat shield at the base of the capsule was stainless steel to endure the 3,000-degree heat of reentry.

My point is, only 3 percent of the beast that left Earth returned to it. And even that command module "gumdrop" was never used again. Can you imagine so much waste?

Then came the Space Shuttle design, which itself was reusable, gliding back to Earth and landing at an airport like an airplane. But it used two huge boosters and a gigantic external fuel tank to get off the planet, all of which were—you guessed it—jettisoned during liftoff. More waste! More space junk! Don't get me wrong. I'm a big fan of those rockets, and we have to remember that was the cutting-edge technology they had back then.

Instead, now, we had ships like the *Aether*, which were designed to take off vertically like a standard rocket. But, unlike the old-school version, these newer designs returned to Earth and landed vertically too. Same for the Minotaur Heavy booster. It was reusable! Reduce, reuse, recycle, right?

The same *Aether* spacecraft and Minotaur Heavy in which we were launching had already flown almost a dozen missions. You could see char marks down the sides.

The *Aether* had even made the trip around the Moon before, but on our particular mission, we would first be stopping over at the International Space Station for a visit. After a little time on station, we'd depart and execute a trans-lunar injection burn (TLI), the all-important boost that would push us on our trajectory to the Moon. Then a stopover at the Gateway outpost circling the Moon to drop off the two mission specialists, then a trip around the rock and back to Earth.

As I thought about this, staring up at our giant hissing rocket ship, I couldn't help but compare it with the SLS. I'd only seen the videos of it launching with Artemis, but what a magnificent treat it would be to experience it firsthand. Eight-point-four million pounds of thrust rattling the earth as it lifted skyward on a plume of white-hot rocket blast. That would be so cool.

I *was* going to launch on this monster right in front of me. I *would* get to experience that feeling, firsthand, while on board. My stomach fluttered.

"Pretty cool, right?" David said, breaking me out of my reverie.

"This is . . . awesome," I said, though even a word like *awesome* didn't capture how truly awe-inspiring it was to be so close to such a force of power and human engineering genius.

I couldn't wait to climb into my saddle at the very tippy top.

"You coming?" Mae shouted from over by the

elevator door. Kal waited inside with her.

David and I moved to join them as quickly as our clunky flight suits would allow.

At the top of the elevator ride, we stepped out into a steel hallway with railings around the edge and a very long drop to the concrete below. I was glad the wind wasn't stronger. Light clouds in the sky. Weather conditions seemed ripe for a liftoff today.

"This is happening," I said to David. He slapped his hands on my chest and my back and did little hops, pumped up with adrenaline even though we still had hours until the final countdown.

The *final* countdown. Wow.

A woman approached in a full-on clean-room suit covering her head to toe—one of those medical-looking outfits that protected us from any germs or dust or extra particles we didn't want on the journey into space.

"Hello, I'm Ashira. I'll help you get into your seats. Your parents are on the next elevator up. But, first, it's a tradition for crew members to make a phone call before boarding." She pointed to a phone on the wall with huge number keys to make it easier to mash the buttons with a flight suit glove.

We were prepared for this. Luckily, the only phone numbers I had memorized were the mobile numbers for my mom and dad.

"I'll go first," I blurted. I kind of wanted to get it over with. After all, what more was there to say? Let's get this show on the road!

The others proceeded down the hall. I could hear Ashira pointing out landmarks in the distance.

After I dialed, the phone rang, and rang, and rang, and just when I thought maybe I'd dialed a wrong number, she picked up.

"Hello?"

"Hi, Mom."

"Fin!" She'd known this call was coming, and yet she still sounded so excited. I grinned, glad she was happy. "Oh, honey, I'm so proud of you."

"I know. Wish you could be here." Why did I say *that*?! Of course she couldn't be here. I bit the inside of my cheek and grumbled.

"I wish I could too. But you and Uncle Dennis are going to have the ride of your life. We'll be watching. I'm so proud of you."

"You already said that."

"And I'll probably say it again. I'm proud of you!"

I laughed.

"Hi, Fin!" It was my dad on speaker.

"Hey, Dad."

"Are you nervous?" my mom asked.

"No, not really, I guess. Just excited. I—" Suddenly,

the question made me think about the saboteur and how Administrator Gould had almost canceled our flight. I remembered Mr. Deuce. I didn't know it was him, but whoever it was—how far would they go to stop this mission? Were we in danger from more than just the explosive rocket?

"Fin?" my dad asked.

"What?"

"You drifted off there. What were you thinking about?"

"Oh, just excited," I said, though it was now mixed with some other feeling.

"What are you most looking forward to?" my mom asked.

"The blastoff. And being weightless. And seeing Earth. And going to the Moon. And, yeah, all of it."

"Drink a water ball for me, okay?" My dad was a goof.

I chuckled. "Okay. Hey, Mom?"

"Yes, honey?"

"How are you feeling?" I hadn't asked her that in a long time. I didn't know why I asked now. I kind of hoped she would give me a lie and say "good" and we could move on.

"I'm good, Fin. Don't worry about me." *Phew.*

"Good, good." I paused. "Well, I gotta go, okay? Love you guys."

"Love you," they chanted in unison.

"Have fun!" my mom said. "We're super proud of you!"

"Bye."

I hung up and walked away, feeling heavier and less enthusiastic than I had before I called. I hate to say it, but I was glad to hang up. I just wanted to get going! It had been so long coming, and now here we were, ready to go.

Kal passed me and smiled. I smiled back, kind of. That helped a little. Beyond Mae and David standing at the railing and gazing out to the distance, the hull of the *Aether* gleamed. The cockpit door stood ajar, beckoning me to come aboard.

I moved swiftly toward my ride.

Chapter 14

Sitting at the top of a metal tube almost 400 feet in the air, nestled on our backs in custom-molded seats aboard the *Aether*, pretty much all I could do was stare out the windows in front of me straight up into the blue Florida sky. I held up my thumb and blocked out the Moon, a thumbnail of waning crescent about to disappear. We'd been waiting for an hour already, with a few more to go.

But I couldn't wait. *Let's get this party started!*

That reminded me of a joke: How do astronauts organize a space party? They planet.

I must have been feeling a bit nervous, because I get chatty and tell jokes when I'm anxious.

On that note, did you know the *Aether* is named after what was called the "upper sky" in Greek mythology? The pure upper air of the gods, as opposed to the "normal" air that we lowly mortals breathe.

Speaking of room to breathe, the *Aether* is spacious.

Not like it was for the three poor sardines who got crammed into the old Russian Soyuz capsule. There were twelve of us in the *Aether*, and there was still tons of space. The huge vessel was built to haul large amounts of cargo, crews for the ISS, or up to fifty space tourists, eventually.

Feeling the purr of the *Aether* as she waited for her big boom, I did contemplate the fact that we were basically sitting on a big bomb about to explode in a semicontrolled chaos of fire and fury. And I was there, voluntarily, willingly, excited and nervous and impatient to hear that final countdown and feel those millions of pounds of thrust *ruuummmbbble* through my body and rattle my brain.

We sat behind the members of the flight crew, who were up near the monitors. We all wore special gloves that made it easier to interact with the touch screens. Dad says there's nothing like the tactile feel of a real metal switch, and I agree, but the touch screens meant that the controls necessary to fly the entire spacecraft were right there on a few monitors and tablets.

Have you seen the cockpit of the space shuttle? That thing had knobs and switches and buttons and levers over the entire ceiling and every square inch of the cockpit!

In the *Aether*, it was much more sparsely decorated. Each of the four flight-crew members had three monitors in front of them and a tablet strapped to their thigh. Each of these displayed different bits of data, charts, video feed, specific controls—whatever they needed to monitor and administer the thousands of sensors and commands needed to get us safely into space.

Seeing as how this was Dr. Sally Sokolov's first blastoff, I made a joke about how this was Sally's first ride, alluding to the famous astronaut Sally Ride.

Mae chuckled, but the joke sort of fell flat. Hey, you win some, you lose some. Of course, the fact that no one laughed made me laugh.

"Get it? Sally's ride?" I tried again.

I got a glance from Commander Horowitz and tried to hold it in, but trying not to laugh when you have a bunch of anticipatory energy is nearly impossible. I kept giggling.

And giggling is, as we all know, highly contagious. Kal caught it next, surprisingly, then it rippled over to David. And, finally, even Mae joined in. Uncle D had no qualms about laughing with us. Then Mae's mom Peggy, and Kal's dad, Rakesh, tittered a bit, hesitating. I think they were the most nervous.

It was fun. We were giddy.

Besides this being Dr. Sokolov's first trip, the other three astronauts had a combined seventeen launches and 344 days in space among them.

Axis Space, and NASA, and our parents—everyone told us we'd be well taken care of on this voyage. At least, they did the best they could.

Chapter 15

With about thirty minutes until liftoff, I couldn't hold my hand steady. I was shaking.

"It's okay to be a little scared, buddy," Uncle D said. Our visors were open so we could communicate directly instead of over the comms, so I snapped my head around to see if anyone had overheard.

"I'm not scared," I whispered back to Uncle D while trying not to move my lips.

"Okay," Uncle D said. He put his head back on the seat rest and stared up. I watched him in profile.

What he'd told me at his house that night I found the Package of Destiny came back to me: *The hardest part is being honest with yourself. Trust me, I know this.*

What did he mean by *I know this*? Uncle Dennis had been on flight missions in the Middle East. What had he dealt with over there?

And yet, here he was, now, with me.

I reached my hand over and laid it on his arm.

"Thanks for being here with me, Uncle D."

"Couldn't have done it without you, Fin." He chuckled.

I guess that was true.

And sure, I was nervous. But I was also extremely excited.

The anticipation was unreal. While I listened and watched our flight crew tick through the final checklists, I kept feeling this surreal, out-of-body experience. Like, was this all a dream? I mean, was I really about to blast off on a giant rocket to space? Really? Me?

I barely blinked because I didn't want to miss a single detail. I knew my heart rate was up; my throat was dry.

Then, over the comms from mission control: "Just a heads-up. We're looking into a potential delay to the launch."

I searched the skies. Some scattered cloud cover, but nothing menacing enough to warrant a launch scrub.

"More info, mission control?" Commander Horowitz asked. I'm sure it was the same thought we all had.

"Possible conjunction for the ISS, so we're in yellow at this time. Please stand by."

"Thank you, mission control. Sounds like nothing to worry about right now, but thanks for keeping us posted," Commander Horowitz replied.

Mae, our space-junk expert, perked up.

"What, Mae?" David asked.

"Yellow. Happens all the time. It's probably nothing. Probably." When we kept staring at her, she continued. "Right. Okay, I'll explain. An Orbital Conjunction Message lights up if the software predicts a probability of collision within a certain threshold of MMOD— that's micrometeoroids and orbital debris—"

Chris, David's dad, interrupted. "Hold, hold. Please. I do not follow." He put his forearm to his brow and wiped the beads of sweat away.

Mae tilted her head away, but I caught her rolling her eyes.

"Can you say again? In English, please?" Chris's English pronunciation was marked by a heavy Norwegian accent, like he twisted his tongue around too much trying to get the words out.

"Explain nicely, Mae," her stepmom said, though it seemed entirely unnecessary to add.

Mae slouched, perhaps consciously to annoy her stepmom.

"Sure." She spread a fake smile, no movement in her eyes. "The US has a Space Surveillance Network that tracks stuff in orbit, but only reliably with stuff that is bigger than ten centimeters." Mae spoke slower this time. "There are something like twenty-five thousand satellites in space. Around the year 2021 there was a huge jump in the number, thanks to a big influx from private companies launching thousands of microsatellites to build Internet frameworks or for other commercial reasons like mapping. But only around 40 percent of those circling the globe are operational. The rest are just dead lumps. And sometimes their batteries or onboard fuel explode, scattering fragments. Then there are the spent rocket stages from all the launches we've done. And sometimes those satellites and space garbage collide— a conjunction—causing more bits and pieces to litter the cosmos. Which is what my StellarKid Project tries to address going forward. All those smaller bits are harder to track. Probably hundreds of millions of tiny pieces that could nonetheless blow a hole right through you before you even realized it. And that's just the human-made junk. Not talking about asteroids or other natural planetary ejecta."

Mae stopped talking. Silence. I was staring at her and imagining a tiny fragment of space junk blasting through me without even seeing it come or go.

Not sure her explanation was helping.

Chris wiped his brow again. "What does that have to do with yellow?"

Mae shook her head as if remembering the original question. "Right. Sorry. Mission control shows a yellow warning for a conjunction at 39.5 hours before TCA on

OCM 5. So let me translate."

"Please," Chris said, sounding impatient.

"Chill, Dad," David remarked out of the side of his mouth. He kind of muttered it under his breath, but we all heard it loud and clear.

Chris batted his eyelids and tightened his lips, but he didn't acknowledge his son's remark.

"Yes, so," Mae continued, "a conjunction means that the surveillance network caught a piece of debris on a *potential* collision course with the ISS. The TCA—time of closest approach—is in 39.5 hours. We'll be up to the ISS in about five hours, if our launch isn't delayed any further. And it's only yellow, meaning it'll probably go green, as most of them do, and then there's nothing to worry about. But some do turn red, or black, which means that the probability of collision is high enough to warrant a debris avoidance maneuver by the ISS. But we'd already be gone from the ISS before they need to conduct that burn, twenty-four hours prior to the potential collision. We might have to leave a little early, or maybe help with the debris avoidance maneuver using the *Aether* thrusters, but—all in all, I agree with the commander. It's nothing we should worry about right now."

"Thank you, Mae," Commander Horowitz chimed in. We all looked forward in surprise; I hadn't thought he was listening. He didn't look back at us, since that would have been difficult from where he was strapped in, but I could imagine his grin. When I looked over at Mae, I could see her cheeks blooming red.

I told you, these are some smart kids.

"Hashtag space junk." Peggy leaned in, looking to her stepdaughter to laugh. Mae gave a "you are ridiculous" sort of look.

Mr. Agarwal chuckled. "Hashtag space junk. That is funny."

"Don't encourage her," Mae groaned.

The comms channel from ground control crackled on. "*Aether*, this is Houston. We've decided to proceed with the launch, but move up the window to give you a little extra time to rendezvous with the ISS, just to be sure you're clear of that OCM 5. Please don your visors and prepare for launch."

"Report systems status, Eileen," Commander Horowitz said, slapping his visor down.

"All systems nominal," Pilot Gurkin replied.

I slid down my visor too. I heard a vacuum seal and knew I was breathing recirculated oxygen in my own little atmosphere. I suddenly felt some toots coming on, but I held it because I knew I'd be the one to suffer in my little isolated bubble.

Chris went to wipe his brow again, but his arm thunked into his visor instead.

"Wait, we're moving the launch *up*?" It was Dr.

Sokolov, fidgeting in her seat. Her first launch.

"Yes, ma'am!" I could sense the big smile on Pilot Gurkin's face.

The chatter at mission control and Houston increased. Not the tone, just the quantity. They never got excited, just like our commander. Always the same flat monotone, as if launching an explosive device off the planet was all in a day's work. Well, for them, I guess it is.

They finished ticking through the final systems checks. Lots of "nominal," which is, of course, good.

Then the famous ten-second countdown began. Finally!

When those Minotaur Heavy main engines fired, the *Aether* on top with us inside started rocking and bouncing. Not a lot, but enough to make me wonder if it was truly nominal or not.

The jostling reminded me of what happens when you shake up a bottle of soda. The *Aether* was the can, and its propellant—the liquid oxygen and liquid methane—was the carbonation, ready to pop.

Unlike the model rockets I'd launch at the park with their sudden burst of takeoff, the Minotaur engines engaged at less than full throttle while things heated up, while the chemicals mixed and exploded below us. Then they increased in power, and the feeling was . . .

I'd describe it as *terrifying magnificence*. I mean, it's

basically a massive semicontrolled explosion (*magnificent*) on top of which I was sitting (*terrifying*). Mostly I was wrapped up in the moment, in the thrill of the raw power.

I held on tight.

The vibration increased. We hadn't even lifted off yet. I heard the countdown hit five.

Mission control was rattling off updates, but it was a blur. Commander Horowitz reached forward and touched a button on his screen, and I wondered how the heck he could control the jitter of his arm right now.

This caged bull was roaring to be let loose, with us as the bull riders.

Then those magic numbers of the *final* countdown.

Three . . . Two . . .

Here we go.

Chapter 16

One!!!

The vibrations steadily increased, wiggling my body in its seat. I kept my jaw clenched, more so out of anxious energy than any fear I'd bite my own tongue.

Here's the odd thing: There was no feeling of *BLASTOFF!* No additional *BOOM.* More like the angry explosion roaring beneath us just got stronger and stronger. I saw on a display up front, in big numbers, that we were actually off the ground and rising steadily. It was a weird illusion because I didn't feel like we'd left Earth; there was no sensation like we were accelerating or moving up.

Yet.

Just as I was marveling at this, I started to feel it. We had burned off enough fuel to really lighten our booster, and that was when it kicked in. And boy, did it kick in!

Oof! Pressed down into my seat, I felt extra heavy. I'd

experienced g-forces in the centrifuge, but this was different. This was like an eight-hundred-pound gorilla sitting on my chest and waggling its haunches around. I could breathe, but my lungs had to work extra hard. My hands gripped the armrests, and I didn't even try to lift my head.

The scattered cloud cover came quick, and we punched through it in a blink.

I heard Mae shout a "woo-hoo!" over the comms. We had our own channel, and I could also hear Houston rattling off metrics like altitude and speed and how far downrange we were, all in that cool, calm voice. I thought I'd be paying more attention to the details, but I lost myself in the experience. Though my ears did perk up whenever I heard a "nominal" amid the chatter. I loved that word now.

I was sure I had a huge freaked-out-but-happy grin plastered across my face. Heck, I blinked free a happy tear or two that streaked back into my ear.

Still accelerating, we had already burst through the sound barrier about thirty seconds into launch and were now flying thousands of feet per second. We had to hit 17,500 miles per hour before we could attain LEO, a low Earth orbit.

"*Aether*, Houston. Pressure differential shows negative delta."

"Copy that, Houston. We're seeing that too. Negative

delta on the pressure differential," Commander Horowitz answered, his voice jumping with his shuddering body.

Something off with the pressure—that didn't sound good.

"*Aether*, Houston. Avionics reports it may be an instrumentation error. Stand by."

"Copy, Houston, standing by."

We were so high up that the blue was turning black. There's never a good time for an accident on your way to space, but being so, so close—I just wanted to get there. To space.

I hoped the next word I heard was NOT *abort*.

"*Aether*, Houston. Instrumentation error confirmed and resolved. Pressure differential reports nominal. Confirm."

"Confirmed, Houston. Pressure nominal."

Phew, that beautiful word again. *Nominal*. Back on track.

"*Aether*, Houston. MECO in ten seconds." I knew this one. Main engine cutoff.

"Copy. MECO."

"Here comes the bump," Pilot Gurkin warned. "In three . . . two . . . one."

Then the engine quit. Immediate silence. I lurched forward against my harness.

"We have MECO," Houston confirmed.

The main Minotaur Heavy booster had shut off. With it, my stomach slid up into my throat.

"And separation in three . . . two . . . one."

A loud pop, and the Minotaur was freed from the *Aether*. The main engine booster would return back to Earth and be reused for the next launch.

A moment later, I was slammed back into my seat when the *Aether* engines fired. That meant we were almost there already, to the Kármán line and officially in outer space. Sixty-two miles—100 kilometers— above the surface.

I'm almost in space, I thought.

For the first *time*, my brain added.

I was hooked. Not even there yet, and already I wanted to go again.

I was one of the first four kids ever to leave the planet.

My arm hairs rose underneath my protective suit. My cheeks ached from the perma-grin.

The screen showed a digital altimeter of our height off the surface of Earth, which was spinning dramatically like it couldn't keep up.

The dimmed lights in our cockpit highlighted the pitch black outside the windows. It reminded me of the black onyx I had in my rock collection. That kind of deep dark that seemed like you could fall into it if you stared too long.

The stars were brilliant-white LEDs against the dark backdrop of the universe. They didn't wink, like you usually see them do because of Earth's atmosphere. They were a solid, bright white light. The sun being the biggest of them all, of course. And it was white too. Not yellow.

Less than a minute later, I heard the commander announce, "There it is. Orbital velocity achieved." That meant we were basically falling in an arc around Earth with enough force to *almost* completely counteract the pull of gravity. We weren't 100 percent out of Earth's loving embrace. If we went any faster, we'd go flying out into the solar system. That tug-of-war between the forces is what would keep us spinning around the planet so we could meet up with the ISS.

That also meant—

"*Aether* engines shutdown in three . . . two . . . one." Pilot Gurkin tapped her screen, and the noise of our fiery entry into space ceased. No fade, it just stopped instantly.

Eleven minutes and some seconds after we'd left Earth, we were now officially in orbit.

The absence of any sound after the turbulent ride up was all-encompassing. I heard my own breathing, my heart pounding.

No one spoke.

Then it hit me.

I did it. Something I'd dreamed of all my life and I was here in outer space.

I felt lighter.

Literally. I was weightless.

I swallowed, which required a little force to do. It made me chuckle. Just giddy, I guess.

It was amazing.

Everyone stared out the windows together, down at Earth skimming below. We were over some stretch of brown land, a desert, laced with a river that reflected the sunlight. I wondered if it was the Nile in Egypt.

Tilting my head up, I could see the horizon and the thin blue line of our atmosphere, no thicker than a layer of water on a bowling ball.

Amazing. I had a feeling I would be repeating that word a lot.

And I must admit, I got a little choked up seeing Earth in that way, for real, in person, right in front of me as one giant whole like never before. I'd seen pictures of this view, but just like photos of the mountains or a beautiful sunset, it's never quite the same as it is in person.

You gotta try it.

I'd read about this inspirational moment, called the overview effect, of seeing fragile Earth from afar, but this time it was *me* experiencing it, personally.

Our precious little blue marble hovering in space

with millions of miles of nothing all around.

I imagined the billions of people below us. The activities and work they were doing, unaware that I was floating right above them, looking down.

Someone hugging their mom before school.

Someone reading a book, snuggled in bed.

Someone drinking water after a hard hike.

Someone crying because their dog ran away.

Someone laughing because their cat licked their nose.

I could see them all below me, in my mind's eye.

It's hard to describe, but it made me feel both large and small at the same time. Like a god's view from the Aether, the upper sky. But instead of feeling like a god, I was reminded more of the people down there, and how I'm just like them, how we're more alike than different. There are no borders visible from space. We're all the same, reaching for the stars. Why?

I remembered something Chris Hadfield said: "When you feel helpless, you're far more afraid than you would be if you knew the facts." Maybe space scares us. It's the great unknown. So, as humans, we want to figure it out. The answers to the universe are up here.

Maybe. Or maybe it's just cool. Or maybe it's both.

Ha. I snorted. It was all a bit too grand for me to fully fathom right at that moment.

Besides, my life down on Earth kind of stank. Who has time to think about the answers to the universe when things at home aren't even right? Getting away from dealing with that drama was all I'd been trying to do since the accident.

Uncle Dennis shoved his head into my field of view and caught my eye with his, a thin smile stretched across his lips, like he knew what I was thinking, like he could see into my head. "That was awesome, right?"

"Amazing," I responded, looking away from him and out the window again.

If it was so amazing, if I'd dreamed of being up here, if I'd yearned to get away from home and my problems there, then why was I thinking about them now? Why did I feel a pang of homesickness?

I gazed down at Earth, which looked so close, and yet so far away.

I thought of my parents. I thought of my mom standing in the kitchen—*standing*—making cookies, while I sat at the table waiting for the fresh ones. Out the back-patio door, I watched my dad, mowing the lawn. Back when things were normal.

Then it turned dark.

My head twitched, and my attention was back in the *Aether*. I looked around, as if someone else might have sensed my daydream. But they were all glued to the view. I considered saying something, but nothing seemed appropriate for the moment, so I continued my silent Earth-watching too.

A sharp line of darkness across the globe indicated the approaching night. Traveling at such a high velocity around the planet, in LEO we'd get a little more than forty-five minutes of dark and -250 degrees Fahrenheit, then about forty-five minutes of sun and 250 degrees. We'd circle the planet in ninety minutes, or about fifteen and a half times per day.

"Welcome to microgravity, kids." Specialist Barrera opened his helmet visor. He spun a round stuffy of the Axis logo, our unofficial microgravity indicator, down the cabin toward us. I followed it as it floated closer to David.

David punched it away, not so playfully, and opened his visor too. He was holding the white barf bag and looking into it like he was examining what he'd packed for lunch. Then he yanked it up to his mouth and retched.

Kal did the same. Her dad looked uneasy, but he wasn't barfing yet.

Dr. Sokolov was quietly gagging into a paper bag too.

My stomach felt fine, luckily, and it looked like the rest of the crew was okay. Or faking it well enough. We were warned that about half of astronauts get Space

Adaptation Syndrome (also known as space motion sickness), but you never hear about that on the news. I guess that on one of the shuttle flights, a diehard jet fighter pilot who never got sick doing barrel rolls and Mach 1 loop-de-loops vomited for so many days that he couldn't perform the duties he had been assigned.

In the earlier days, poor Jake Garn was so violently ill that the Astronaut Corps, and now NASA, still measures space sickness by the Garn scale. And that guy had logged 17,000 hours flying military aircraft! He hadn't exhibited any symptoms during training on the "vomit comet" airplane that simulates zero g. Poor guy. What a thing to be famous for.

By my estimation, David looked like he was at about half a Garn, but I'm no expert.

Whatever his rating, it was weird to see big, strong David quivering and heaving his guts into a bag. I had to look away when I saw a chunk float from him. Gross!

I mean, glad it wasn't me. I thought I should probably wait a little while, but for sure I'd be teasing him about that later.

His dad put a hand on David's back and said something directly to him. I couldn't hear, because our visors were open now and comms were off, but David shrugged his shoulder and pushed his dad's arm away.

And poor Kal. She'd stopped puking and was

leaning back in her chair with her eyes closed, gripping the armrests like she was spinning and wanted it to stop. Her helmet was off and floating next to her. Her dad grabbed for it but accidentally knocked it across the cockpit instead.

"I got it," Uncle D said, pulling the helmet close to his chest.

And then I heard the next set of words, which I had been waiting for.

Commander Horowitz said, "You are free to move about the cabin. About thirty minutes until rendezvous with the ISS, so stretch your legs. And I have to apologize. There will be no peanuts served on this flight."

I was a little surprised at the cheesy joke from the hardened aviator, but I chuckled through my teeth. I was already pushing out of my seat by the time he finished.

Playtime.

Chapter 17

I did a few obligatory flips, played with the stuffy, laughed with the others, and even did Michael Jackson's moonwalk on the wall (sorry, not sorry, had to do it). Then I went back to staring out the window. There'd be more time to play in microgravity, but right now the view was irreplaceable. Plus, we were about to fly over the Pacific Northwest of the US, and I wanted to find my house.

David and Kal, still clipped into their jump seats with eyes closed, had barf bags at the ready.

"If you don't move your head," Pilot Gurkin explained, "the vestibular system in your inner ear won't conflict as much with what your visual input is expecting. That disparity between what your balance says should be happening—falling—versus what your eyes see—not falling—makes your brain go haywire."

"Why do our brains think throwing up will help?" I asked.

David grunted and told me to be quiet through clenched teeth, in less-than-polite terms. Kal actually chuckled at that one, but then gagged.

Mae's curly hair was splayed out all around her head like a lion's mane after an electric shock, so she tied it back with a red rubber band. I couldn't help but notice her case of "space face"—the strained look when the fluids in a body redistribute and make the person look puffy. One vein on her forehead popped like she was lifting weights. She caught me staring, which forced me to pretend I was actually just stargazing out the window behind her, away from Earth and out into deep space.

The field of pinpoint stars was static except for one bright object that seemed to be getting bigger the closer we got to it. Pretty quickly, it took on more of a shape and revealed more depth, becoming a three-dimensional bug with all sorts of arms and tubes and big golden dragonfly wings that reflected the sunlight.

As we pulled even closer, it kept growing in size.

The International Space Station.

The length of a football field (American football, Mae was quick to correct) with modules sticking out all over the place, it's like this floating desert oasis out in the void of space.

I pointed to the module at the back. "Russian Zarya. The first piece delivered last century. In 1998."

Uncle Dennis turned from his view of Earth and followed my gaze.

"And there's Unity," I continued, amazed it was really right in front of me. Like, for real. "The first American module."

"The other primary habitat modules were tacked on over the course of a dozen years," Specialist Barrera added.

I could name each one and fly in my mind's eye through every corner of the station because I'd done that on my computer via Google Earth's 360 augmented-reality simulator.

But I couldn't wait to experience it firsthand. I was so close to boarding the ISS, for real.

What's really wild is that the ISS had been continuously occupied since the year 2000. That meant that, for the past twenty-six years, there have been multiple people floating around in space high above your head down on Earth.

Look up. Even right now, there are humans up there. Someone may be sleeping, or fixing the toilet, or conducting a science experiment. In space, right at this very moment.

Meanwhile, we coast through our lives unaware that this vessel is up there, always working and humming and zipping around the planet. This is not science fiction or the future. This outpost has been staffed for longer than I've been alive. I'm sure you've looked up at the night sky, maybe identified a satellite moving through the stars, and every time you did, there could have been people looking right back at you.

The international space agencies, working together, still delivered new pieces to the ISS here and there, but that heavy lifting was now provided mostly by commercial companies like Axis. Most of NASA's exploration effort and money were currently spent on expanding the Gateway outpost orbiting the Moon, part of the overall Artemis project. Besides offering a hub for lunar exploration, Gateway could be used as a way station and refueling depot for missions to Mars.

Gateway is the future. The ISS is the past. At least, as far as NASA's primary focus is concerned.

Although, in LEO, there are also private space stations being constructed. The "commercialization of space" they call it, for tourists like me. And you, someday, probably. There are also the Chinese and Russian stations.

But, for NASA, which serves as the tip of the spear in human space exploration, the focus is on Gateway, the Moon, and Mars.

A global sense of pride at what we little humans have accomplished tickled my neck, and I puffed out my chest as I watched our final approach to the ISS. In that moment, I recognized my place as a tiny piece of the grander puzzle, a few lines in that ongoing epic of human space travel.

I expected that visiting the ISS would be more like a trip to a museum, to pay our respects to the brave people who paved the way for where I was today.

In the simplest of terms, you can think of the US segments of the ISS as a giant capital *I* with a crossbar at the top and bottom, laid flat, parallel to Earth. The US segments are joined to the Russian segments, but we didn't get to tour those, so I'll just give you a quick rundown of the US portion.

At the front of the station, the *I* crossbar is composed of the European and Japanese modules as the arms on each side, connected by the US Harmony module in the middle. The main part of the *I* trunk is the US Destiny module, the main scientific lab. At the bottom of the *I* junction is the original US Unity module, which connects to the arms of the Quest air lock on one side and the Tranquility module on the other. Tranquility is where the cupola is, the 360-degree windows that look down on Earth.

There's more to it than what I described, of course, but those are the basics.

The huge truss assembly, like giant towers of scaffolding laid across the top of the station, hold gigantic solar arrays. The solar panels are a bit of a patchwork quilt, having been expanded and upgraded several times over the years as the technology became more efficient. They generate the electricity to power all the necessary machines to allow humans to live in the vacuum of space, and to conduct science experiments, chat on the Internet, etc. Hanging from support beams stretch all kinds of boxes and antennas and such, like those droid scouts from *The Empire Strikes Back*.

The whole ISS may be huge, the solar panels alone covering an acre, but the total living and working space on the ISS is about the same volume as on a 747 airplane you might take on a cross-country trip. Imagine living on an airplane for a year, and you might start to understand why Scott Kelly and Mikhail Korniyenko were so ready to come home after their year up there! No showers either!

The orientation of the ISS is described using terms you'd hear on a boat: *forward* for the front, *aft* for the back, *port* for the left, and *starboard* for the right. I can never remember port from starboard, but my mom taught me a trick. *Port* has four letters, and so does *left*.

Why don't they just say "the left side"? Who knows. Ask the mariners.

You'll also hear them using *nadir* for the bottom and *zenith* for the top. So, the Tranquility module with the cupola, for example, is on the port side of the ISS, and the cupola is on the nadir of Tranquility, pointing down to Earth.

But that's a lot of detail to chew on. Sorry, I tend to like details. If you want to be an astronaut, you have to.

"*Aether*, this is ISS. PMA-3 on the zenith is occupied, so you'll dock with PMA-2 forward."

"Copy, ISS. Green for docking PMA-2 forward. See you soon," Commander Horowitz confirmed.

As we approached, Pilot Gurkin's hands were millimeters away from the manual joystick controls, ready to take over in a heartbeat if something went wacky with the automated system.

We hushed as if we were watching a daring circus act. I was definitely holding my breath. The docking is one of the most dangerous parts of space travel, aside from launch and reentry. These ships aren't built like tanks. They don't need to be. Plus, every gram adds to the upmass—the weight the rocket has to push out of gravity's hold. So, if you hit the docking port at the wrong angle, you could tear a hole in your hull, or the ISS, and that would be bad. Like, sucked-into-the-vacuum-of-space bad.

I flashed back to Mae's failed simulation, the one that was probably rigged, probably by Deuce.

My palms suddenly felt damp.

But, of course, Pilot Gurkin was cool, not even a hint of nerves. She probably wasn't considering the possibility of getting sucked into space because of the interference of an Evil Accountant, and instead she just focused on the task at hand, for which she'd trained a thousand times. "And docking in three . . . two . . . one."

Clunk.

The docking mechanism on the nose of the *Aether* slid gently into the receptor, and we heard a metallic *chunk-chunk-chunk* as the bolts twisted into place, securing us to the International Space Station.

"We show a good dock, *Aether*," the ISS radioed.

We were really there!

David and Kal both had their eyes open and were doing their best to muscle through the nausea. I'm sure they didn't want to miss this for anything.

Kal gave me an odd smile. I nodded.

"Glad you're feeling better," I said.

"Yes, fine," she said. "I'm fine. It's fine."

Okay, that was obviously not true.

Commander Horowitz twisted open our side of the porthole, and three smiling ISS crew members greeted us warmly: Commander Valentina Smith, Flight Engineer Charles Morales, and Science Officer Christa Allaire. It was like seeing rock stars in person.

The commander of the *Aether* and the commander of the ISS did the traditional handshake within the threshold of the ISS before we could cross—the

Russians believed it was bad luck to enter before greeting each other, and the tradition stuck. Then they let us kids through next.

"We come bearing gifts," I said, as practiced, holding out a bag of crisp Fuji apples.

Mae slid up alongside me, offering, with two hands, a huge sack of multicolored carrots. "Hope you like fresh veggies!"

"Yum!" Engineer Morales snatched at the fruit and vegetables greedily. "I've been up here for three months, and I'm dying for some fresh food besides the spindly lettuce Christa is growing. Sorry, Christa, no offense."

"Ah, that's okay," Officer Allaire said. "I won't tell it you said that."

We chuckled.

Then they ushered us inside the hallowed sanctum of the International Space Station.

Chapter 18

Science Officer Christa Allaire—"Call me Christa," she insisted—gave us kids a guided tour of the ISS. The ISS commander, Valentina Smith, took the adults, since there wasn't really enough room for us all to be in the same place at the same time.

Christa was a short woman, shorter than me. She wore a big Garmin watch, and I got the sense she ran marathons or triathlons back on Earth. She had brown eyes and curly brown hair that bounced as she floated through the station. Christa came from England and wore the European Space Agency (ESA) badge on her black polo shirt. A thin gold chain with a pendant of someone's initials danced lazily around her neck. When the necklace bobbed up into her face, she blew it away, gently.

I mostly listened as she gave the tour, practically in shock that I was actually, really there, for real. We entered through the Harmony module from our docking point, and Christa led us into the ESA module, Columbus, to our left. She smiled and touched the walls of science experiments tenderly, like they were her babies. She showed us the lettuce. And then I learned what *spindly* meant; the lettuce was tall and skinny, not like the big leafy greens we grow under gravity. But fresh greens in any form, for the vitamins they provide, and the carbon dioxide they convert to oxygen, are an important part of our travel plans to Mars, or if we want to maintain any sort of permanent base on the Moon.

I wondered if we could grow an apple tree on the Moon. Why apple, you wonder? I don't know. I like apples.

Across from Columbus on the other side of Harmony was Kibo, the Japanese module. Beyond that, out in space and not visible to us, was a special collection of experiments that required a vacuum.

That concluded the top of the *I* crossbar tour. Now down into the trunk, moving aft, we entered the main lab, the Destiny module, the biggest node. Besides a lot of experiments and wires and cables, it housed the sleeping quarters for four astronauts. By "sleeping quarters," I mean rectangular holes only slightly bigger than coffins. They were in a ring on the floor, the walls, and the ceiling, with a thin door you could Velcro shut for a little privacy. Christa demonstrated the sleeping-bag thing they attached to the wall to sleep in, arms floating in front of her in a sort of creepy, zombielike way. It sank in, perhaps for the first time for real, that I'd be sleeping in that way too, albeit on the *Aether*. The sleep cabins on the *Aether* were bigger than the ones on the ISS, by about double, but still pretty modest.

Christa also demonstrated the stationary bike in the Destiny module. David seemed interested in trying it out too, and she let him hop on. I was shocked, given his pale face, but David is an avid athlete, so I guess I shouldn't have been surprised. And his StellarKid Project submission was about making exercise in space more fun and less boring with augmented-reality video games, so of course he wanted to jump on to try the real deal. Well, jump "on" was not quite right, because it had no seat! No reason to sit in space. There were no chairs anywhere. Odd to consider a completely new way to live for these people. No sitting or lying down for weeks or months at a time.

David pedaled somewhat awkwardly, bouncing around. Christa, not trying to hide her grin at David's exuberance, explained that the stationary bike floated freely and had a system for controlling the vibrations, because if it was attached to the actual structure of the vessel, someone getting a good workout like David was (we snickered) would push their kinetic energy into the ship and potentially affect delicate scientific experiments.

"Especially David," Mae teased. "Big oaf."

"Hey, you try!" David teased back. He used that as an excuse to dismount. His face was looking a bit flushed, but that was better than the washed-out pale it had been before.

"There's also a treadmill and a weight-lifting machine called the ARED—for Advanced Resistive Exercise Device—down in the Tranquility module, but we'll see those in a minute." Christa gestured farther aft.

We left the Destiny module, the main trunk of the *I*, and headed toward the junction with the Unity node.

"This is Unity, one of the oldest modules," Christa said, glancing around the small space.

As I floated next to Christa, I inspected the famous Unity module with a reverence most people would reserve for cathedrals or art museums. I was in awe, but I couldn't stop from also thinking: *Wow, Unity shows signs of its age.*

The walls had this slightly yellow or light tan tint, like what a smoker's lungs look like. I mean, it *was* a tiny metal cylinder that had had people living, breathing, and sweating in it for over twenty-five years. Renovations there were very difficult. Gray duct tape literally held things together. Every square inch of the space was covered. Notes handwritten in Sharpie, random equipment such as scissors, pens, or cables—all sorts of stuff. It was cluttered, not at all like the austere cleanliness of our more modern *Aether*.

And despite the crowded little crumbling old space, or probably *because of* the knickknacks and the history literally stained into the walls, I couldn't help but consider this hallowed ground. Or hallowed *space*.

I was floating where so many famous astronauts had been. I reached and put my hand on the wall, my fingers splayed out like I was feeling a living, breathing creature. It gently purred beneath my palm, and I swear I felt a heartbeat.

"Unity is also the mess hall, where we eat," Christa continued. "Of course, there are no stoves or ovens. Open flame is a big no-no in a sealed, oxygen-rich environment like this." She took a silver package that looked like a heavy-duty Ziploc bag from one of the cubbies. "All food and drink is dehydrated, so we just have to add water through this little spout, shake it up a bit, and bon appétit. No cooking and very little cleanup."

Sounds easier than at home, where I have to do the dishes three nights a week. I could be okay with recyclable pouches for dinner on my dishes nights.

Christa put the bag back in its spot and pointed behind me, to the starboard side of the station. "Over here, we have the Quest air lock. Before this component was installed, space walks could be done only when the shuttle was visiting or from the Russian side, from the Zvezda, using Russian Orlan space suits, because the American EMUs don't fit over there."

This seemed silly to me. The American and Russian suits used different connecter configurations. Seems like an engineering mistake, but I'm sure it wasn't an accident. The US wanted bigger space suits, I guess, so we built our own air lock too. That's kind of how we roll.

Two space suits stood in the equipment-room portion of the air lock like ghosts, with sacks over their heads. Beyond the suits was a smaller chamber called the crew lock, barely big enough for two astronauts in space suits to squish into together.

"The astronauts are sealed in here before the air is sucked out to match the vacuum of space, a process called depressurization," Christa explained. "But first, to prepare for a space walk—or an EVA, as we know NASA likes to call it, for extravehicular activity— astronauts have to purge their bodies of nitrogen. If they don't, they could get 'the bends.' The same problem a scuba diver who ascends too rapidly may experience. It's technically called decompression sickness. It happens when the nitrogen bubbles inside your body expand, which can cause all sorts of problems—from a few joint aches, to fever, even to stroke and death in some cases. It's serious. But it's easy to avoid if you take the right precautions."

"Sounds nasty," I said.

"It can be," Christa replied. "But with proper preparation, it's no big deal at all. And if it does occur, the solution is simple."

"What's it like in the space suit?" Mae asked.

Christa put her hand in one of the gloves and squeezed her fingers a few times. "When the astronauts are in their EMU, they're not fully pressurized the same as you are right now by the atmosphere around you. If they pressurized the suit that much, it would be so rigid that they wouldn't be able to bend their arms and legs. To prepare for that depressurization, and to rid their bodies of nitrogen, astronauts have some options. They can breathe pure oxygen and exercise for hours before the space walk, or they can camp out overnight in the sealed-off Quest air lock with a reduced-nitrogen atmosphere, while they steadily lower the atmospheric pressure pushing on their body. Both approaches rid the body of nitrogen."

"You mean you can't just throw on a suit and leap into space whenever you want?" I asked.

Christa chuckled and smiled. "No, sorry, not that simple."

I knew that; it was a joke.

Anyway, that waiting must be boring. I would be

super impatient crammed inside that tiny tube and just *waiting* to go walk in space. Let me out!

"Once that preparatory work is done and the spacewalkers are ready, they open a hatch that points to the nadir side of the station, straight down at our planet whisking by below," she explained.

I'd heard it was quite an experience stepping out into the nothingness. I couldn't imagine it.

"It does take a leap of faith to let go of the ship your first time," Christa said. I knew she'd spacewalked several times. "Your primal brain is telling you that you're going to fall and die. But well-trained astronauts know it's an optical illusion and push through that pesky voice of fear. They acknowledge the fear, but don't give in to it." She paused and looked each of us in the eye, obviously wanting us to acknowledge some sort of imparted wisdom.

"Cool," David said.

I sighed, thinking about what an awesome test that would be, to step into the void. I wanted to go out there so bad, and I was bummed I wouldn't get to try a space walk during this trip. That's what they'd told me back in training at JSC, no matter how much I pleaded and reasoned. I was still going to try to persuade the commander to give us some outside time. After I successfully demonstrated the prototype SAFER attached to my custom-made EMU, in the protected confines of the *Aether*, of course.

The *Aether* had an air lock and decompression chamber about midway down the giant tube from our main cockpit. It was stocked with two space suits as standard equipment in the event that any midflight inspections or repairs were required. That was standard procedure for crewed *Aether* flights. We also carried my custom EMU, just to test the SAFER prototype.

"Are we going down there?" Kal asked, pointing toward a narrow passageway heading farther aft from Unity. She looked nervous about the prospect of shimmying through the tiny passage.

"Through there is the Russian segment, but we're not going to tour that right now. Maybe later," Christa said.

Kal looked relieved.

"Aw, I was hoping to see the original Zvezda module," Mae said.

"And Zarya," David added.

"Sorry, kids, but they have the porthole closed right now for some internal procedures, and we can't disturb them." Christa held her hands out in a gesture of *sorry*. "But, like I said, maybe later. Sounds like you already know they have their own bathroom, mess hall, and exercise equipment, as well as their own science experiments."

"And the Zvezda module has the thruster for course corrections when the station needs it," Mae added.

"That's right. Zvezda is an important node," Christa agreed.

"When do you think we'll get to see it?" Mae asked.

"I'm not sure," Christa said. "The Zvezda has the only other windows in the ISS, but they're tiny compared with the cupola. Want to see?"

I nodded my head vigorously.

Still floating in Unity, Christa spun around from facing the Quest air lock to look in the opposite direction, to the port side. "The Tranquility module. My favorite." She smiled.

"This node has the ARED machine for working out, which looks like some sort of forklift. There's also a treadmill in here," Christa said, pointing to the wall.

It was so weird to think that someone could be "lifting" weights on one surface while another person was literally running up the wall perpendicular to them.

Tranquility also had a bathroom—at which we took turns sneaking a peek. I held my nose, but it only smelled like disinfectant wipes anyway. We knew we'd have to use it sooner or later. The *Aether* might be more modern, but the waste-recycling system was basically the same technology.

"As I think you know," Christa said, detecting our

interest, "that little unit is responsible for processing the urine and wastewater several times over until it is clean enough to drink. In fact, without the water-recovery system, the ISS crew would need a lot more water hauled up from Earth. And water is heavy, aka a lot of upmass. It already costs a lot of money per kilogram to get stuff off of Earth and to the ISS. But besides all the money saved, instead of hauling water we can transport more science experiments or other supplies for the ship that are not as easily extracted from our own urine."

She smiled in a cheesy way. "It sounds gross, I know, but the filtration system is built by very talented engineers, so the water is actually cleaner than the stuff that comes out of your tap. Think about that."

I did not want to think about that.

Christa pushed herself into the Tranquility module. "I present to you the best part of the station, the cupola." She looked "down" at the floor. We huddled closer to her.

On the nadir side of the station, the cupola extended toward Earth with a 360-degree view.

"Amazing," I said.

The windows in the *Aether* had wowed me, but this expansive view from the cupola took my breath away. It was the closest you could get to actually being out there, without worrying about depressurization.

When I flipped my body around and stuck my head down into the cupola, I saw we were over an ocean with lots of clouds.

"It's pretty common to see the ocean, since that's most of what Earth is," Christa said. Not quite in a whisper, but she now spoke with that gentle hush we reserve for special moments.

Skimming past the scene, the imagined sensation of movement suddenly made me wobble, as if my head couldn't quite understand what was happening.

I closed my eyes and saw a sizzling flash of light.

My eyes snapped open, and I inhaled a quick shot of air, surprised. I looked around. No flashing lights, no damage. "Did you guys see that? That flash?"

"A faint burst, kind of at the edge of your vision?" Christa jiggled her fingers at the side of her head.

"Yes," I said, wiggling my fingers near my temple. "What was that?"

"Probably a cosmic ray. High-energy particles ejected from some distant star eons ago. And aren't you lucky it just zipped right through your optic nerve? Starlight."

"Starlight. Is that bad?" I asked. "Like, radiation?"

"Good question. But no, not that we know of. A lot of astronauts have reported the experience, and no negative effects have ever been documented."

I noticed how she appended that caveat, "have ever

been documented." Not sure that made me feel entirely better, but at least she seemed calm about it.

I pushed up out of the cupola to give Mae a turn; only about two people could fit in there comfortably.

While moving past the bathroom, I got another whiff of cleaning detergent, and this time my mind raced back to the hospital after the accident.

The ISS in general had given me this hospital-like vibe. I mean, it was clean and tidy, yet also cluttered, if that makes sense? Like a hospital. There were no windows (except the cupola); the lighting was bright white, sort of like those annoying flickering overhead bulbs; and there's this constant whirring noise of fans and machinery. I could practically hear the beeping of the heart monitor.

It also had that same sense of . . . fragility. Like it'd always been there, but maybe someday it wouldn't be. Like my mom.

I clenched my jaw at the memory of sitting in the bright hospital room, that cleaning-solution smell, all those wires and tubes connected to the person who'd always been there for me—

I didn't want to think about that right now. Or ever, if I could help it.

Crack. What was that?

Crack. The muffled sound of a rifle shot outside, but that couldn't be.

"What?!" Kal's body jolted from the surprise, and she threw her hand onto her chest.

"No need to fret," Christa said soothingly. "That's completely nominal. As expected, I mean. Metal expands and contracts as we get hotter and colder diving in and out of sunlight and shadow as we circle Earth. Nothing to worry about."

Kal's eyes darted around, apparently not satisfied with that explanation.

A faint buzz.

Christa looked at her watch. She pursed her lips and nodded her head in thought, as if she'd just received distressing news. "Excuse me," she said, then pushed past and started tapping on a laptop nearby.

Over her shoulder, I could see a blinking update on OCM 5, the Orbital Conjunction Message about space debris we'd received while waiting on the launchpad. The one that had been yellow.

Only now it was red.

Chapter 19

Red is a pretty universal indicator of "not good," so I admit I had a moment of anxiety about what might happen next. I think we've already established that hypervelocity space debris could be very bad for an aging aluminum can held together by duct tape. I knew what Mae had told us about a debris avoidance maneuver and how this sort of thing was relatively routine. The ISS did several of these a year out of an abundance of caution.

But still. A scrap of metal zipping at us with so much energy could puncture the hull and depressurize a module, or worse. Hopefully, it'd be a small hole and we'd have time to react. Maybe we could repair it. Or, if the puncture was bigger, we could close the hatch to the damaged node and seal it off before it imploded the rest of the station. But either way, it'd definitely put a damper on the trip. What if it cut us off from our exit? Or if it damaged the *Aether*, and we were stuck here.

Or if it pierced right through one of us?

Okay, stop the mental tornado, I told myself. Christa's focus helped me shake off the what-ifs and assess the situation for what it was. We were safe. This was a routine situation for these experienced professionals. We were in good hands.

I realized that all the adults besides Christa were hanging out over in the mess hall in Unity and in the Quest air lock. Rakesh was slurping from a round sphere of water floating in front of him, laughing giddily. They didn't seem to have noticed the warning.

"I don't feel so good," David said, popping up from the cupola. I suspected that looking out that window might have reawakened his space sickness. "I'm gonna head back to the *Aether* and close my eyes."

Mae said she'd go too and thanked Christa for the tour. Christa smiled politely and gave a wave of her hand without looking up from the laptop. A big set of calculations and procedures scrolled by on the screen. I thought maybe she was reviewing the burn procedure Houston had sent up for the avoidance maneuver.

I wanted to tell Mae. She would be interested in this. But when I turned to say something to her, I saw David curl over, and she put her arm around his waist as they departed down Destiny toward the *Aether*. I hoped David could hold his vomit.

Kal said she'd head back to the *Aether* too.

When I didn't immediately respond, Kal gave me the stink eye and gestured toward David. Like I'm his babysitter? "Looks like Mae is taking care of the big guy," I said.

"I think we should go," Kal said. Then, with her eyes and a flick of her head, she looked to Christa and motioned away, suggesting we leave Christa to do her important work.

Okay, I guess that made sense. "Uh, yeah."

We weren't technically scheduled to undock for another couple of hours, but maybe with a debris avoidance maneuver on the way for the ISS, we should prepare for an early departure. We had known our visit would be short anyway. The ISS life-support system was designed to handle only seven crew members on a regular basis. And given that there were twelve of us newcomers, I was sure we were taxing the systems.

I stopped as I passed out of Tranquility and through Unity to chat with Uncle Dennis about what he'd seen. Then I let him know we were heading back to the much more spacious *Aether*.

"I hear ya," he said. "I think we're gonna hang out here a bit longer, soak it up while we can, but we'll be there soon." Uncle Dennis gave a squeeze to my shoulder.

Specialists Barrera and Sokolov were bent over a shoebox-size container Velcroed to the table in the

Unity module, peering inside while Engineer Morales pointed and explained something about carbon dioxide filtration.

Over in the Quest air lock area, Commander Horowitz had his fist to his chin and was conferring with his pilot, Captain Gurkin, and Commander Smith.

Behind me, back in Tranquility, the three parents—Rakesh, Peggy, and Chris—crowded toward the cupola. They were bouncing off one another and clearly didn't acknowledge that only two, at most, could fit in the viewing area at the same time.

Christa was still tapping on her keyboard, so deep in thought she didn't notice the comical scene of the parents jostling around. I floated at the edge of the module, watching her, trying to read her face. She still looked concerned, but focused. Not worried, maybe, but not the eager, smiley schoolteacher she'd acted like while giving our tour.

The adults will handle it, I thought. Little did I know.

Chapter 20

With both arms straight out in front of me like Superman, I flew down Destiny, sailed through the Harmony junction, and whizzed past the narrow PMA-2 dock into the *Aether*. I couldn't imagine that would ever get old.

"Hey, look at me!" I threw my fist forward, as if I were accelerating, at the exact same instant as—

BOOM!!!!

My eardrums popped from the extremely loud pressure wave. Then there was a *whoosh* like a tornado pulling on every inch of my body. Alarms blared to life. Red lights strobed. I was getting sucked back toward the docking port connecting the *Aether* with the station.

The ISS had had some sort of catastrophic depressurization. My arms instinctively flung outward and landed on the metal ridges at either side of the circular porthole. I latched on and managed to avoid getting pulled out of the *Aether*, but the force of the suction was strong, and my feet were flopping around beneath me, useless with nothing to push against.

And the noise! The screaming-teakettle whistle of the air evacuating was terrible. Wind whipped through my hair, but I knew there could be no wind here. That was our oxygen rushing out into the vacuum.

I had to close the hatch between the *Aether* and the damaged station, or we'd be goners. But I was dangling out of the opening, with more of my body in the hobbled station than in the *Aether*.

I had to get back into our ship.

I pulled with all my strength and inched forward. It was like a pull-up with dumbbell weights wrapped around my body.

I couldn't hold it. I flopped back down, and one hand slipped off. I was dangling by one arm.

My fingers were sweaty and slipping, and I yelped, but I could barely hear myself. The air was getting thinner and not carrying the sound waves. Sparkles danced in my eyes.

I dared not look backward. I didn't want to see the hole I'd get sucked into if I let go. I didn't have the energy anyway.

My fingers gripping the hatch door slipped again. I couldn't hold on much longer.

This was it . . . The metal slipped out of my hold.

In that same millisecond, someone grabbed my

wrist. Their palm was sweaty too, but it was a lifeline. I looked up through speckled vision and saw David. Behind him, Mae was holding around his waist. She had a strap of some kind wrapped around her and David's waists to keep them from getting sucked out. We were dangling together.

I didn't know how long David's grip could hold me, but I hoped his experience in gymnastics would come in handy.

David and Mae yanked and squirmed and eventually pulled me far enough into the *Aether* that I could stand on the porthole. Then I was all the way into the *Aether*. The sucking force had lessened. My ears were still plugged and breathing was difficult, but the terrible suction had weakened.

The alarms still blared, but muffled. The lights strobed.

Kal launched from across the cabin, palms forward, and slammed into the *Aether* door's stowage latch. I could see her grunting when she yanked on it, but she sounded so far away. Her effort released the door, and the hatch automatically swung shut.

But it didn't settle in properly. The escaping air now whistled through a narrow sliver, and that teakettle shrieked again. Kal pushed at the door to try to close it completely, but it didn't budge.

David, Mae, and I jumped to help and bonked into

one another. David made it first and heaved his shoulder into the door.

It thunked shut. Thank goodness.

The steam-whistle noise ceased immediately, though the alarms still blared.

"Emergency pressurization procedure commencing." It was the *Aether*'s almost-British voice informing us that it would automatically correct for the lost air by refilling our cabin from the reserve canisters.

Mae twisted the ratchet handle on the *Aether*'s hatch door. We heard the bolts lock into place.

My heart pounded. My throat was dry. But with each passing second, my vision returned. I could breathe again.

Kal turned off the alarms. "What happened?!" she cried out, breathing heavily too.

This time, I heard her just fine. I'd never seen her so rattled. But then again, we all probably looked that way after the disaster that had just occurred.

"Space debris?" Mae questioned, shaking her head back and forth like she couldn't believe that was the answer. "They said we had time. They said the TCA was still—"

"Guess they got it wrong," David said. He still had his hand on the hatch, looking through the tiny viewport to the other side.

Uncle Dennis. The parents. Commander Horowitz

and Specialist Barrera and Dr. Sokolov. Christa and the ISS crew.

We looked at one another, obviously thinking the same thing.

Were they gone?

The possibility was too awful to consider.

"They're fine," I said, probably too quickly.

"How do you know?" Kal choked out.

"Because I just do. They're fine." I couldn't deal with this. I came up here to get away from my problems at home, not add to them. They had to be fine. This was easy to fix. It had to be. Life had already been unfair to me. I didn't deserve any more torture.

A crackle came over the speakers in the *Aether* cabin. "*Aether*, come in. This is the ISS. Repeat. *Aether*, come in. ISS here." It was Commander Horowitz, characteristically cool.

Kal smashed her hand on the button to talk. "Yes, we're here! We almost got sucked out, but—is—is my dad okay?" She stuttered as if she were afraid to ask the question.

"We're all here," David added. "We're okay."

"Roger that," the commander responded. I thought something a little more celebratory was called for, but I noticed he didn't answer Kal's question about her dad. "Everyone here is okay too."

There it was. They were *fiiiine*.

I let out a breath. Uncle D was okay. They were all okay. Mae and Kal hugged. David ran a hand through his hair and exhaled like he was blowing out a candle.

"But we had to seal off the Harmony module," the commander continued. The Harmony module was our junction to the station. With that blocked off, we were effectively cut off from the ISS.

"And, per protocol, we fled to the central post for emergency operations."

"Zvezda," Mae said.

"The Russian command module." Kal looked down, like she was thinking or remembering something.

The commander continued. "We had to batten down the hatches as we retreated, to ensure that no other modules would be compromised. So that means that the *Aether* is separated from the rest of the ISS by a depressurized Harmony module."

"What happened?" Mae asked. "The debris wasn't scheduled to cross our trajectory this early, right?"

"We don't know," Commander Horowitz answered. "Houston is working the problem."

Gotta love the honesty. Part of me sort of missed the old days when I was a younger kid, when adults would tell me little white lies to save me from hard feelings.

Yes, honey, everything is going to be fine, my mom had said from her bed in the hospital. She'd lied.

Now I wanted the truth. "What's the plan?" I asked.

"Just sit tight," the commander answered.

"But if it was debris," Mae said, "it's going to come around again in orbit. Depending on its velocity and trajectory, we might have maybe another ninety minutes before it hits again."

"Or it could be days." It was Pilot Gurkin talking now. "*If* it was debris."

"She's right," the commander said. "We don't know what we don't know. So while Houston works the problem, we should focus on what we *can* control. Our first challenge is to stabilize our orbit."

"What do you mean, 'stabilize our orbit'?" Mae asked.

"The ISS has taken on a wobble from that blast. The rapid unplanned evacuation of atmosphere from Harmony served as a boost to knock us cattywampus, and with that external thrust we experienced a negative delta-vee. Thus, our orbit is degrading."

I think I followed that. Sounds like we were tilting. And delta-vee is the change in velocity, so a negative delta-vee would mean we'd slowed down a little, which meant our giant arc around Earth was now more shallow than it should have been. We could slip down into the lower atmosphere, where the friction would tear us apart.

"That could be a good thing here," Pilot Gurkin said.

A good thing?

"We'd be out of the same orbit as whatever hit us," Mae said, pointing her index finger in the air.

"*If* something hit us," David added.

I thought of the sabotaged centrifuge and Mr. Deuce. He wouldn't do something as sinister as this, though, would he?

"What else could it be?" Kal turned to a screen and started tapping on one of the keyboards. Her deliberate actions made me think that she already had an idea what it could have been.

"You looking for something?" I asked, peering over her shoulder.

"I'm sure Houston won't mind the help." She shrugged, a little too casually.

"But you guys," David said. He paused, then looked at each of us. "If we're going down, won't we just burn up in the atmosphere?"

Kal's fingers tapped around on the display and she brought up a screen that said:

MOTION CONTROL SYSTEM — CONTROL MOMENT GYROSCOPES

Below that, it had several indicator lights. All of them were red.

"That can't be good," David said. *No kidding.*

"It's too much attitude loss." Mae pointed to a different output, a graphic of a sphere with x, y, and z

coordinates. Each number designated our position relative to our target alignment. They were all negative. We were off course. A ghost diagram of the station overlaid on a blueprint indicating the desired attitude showed that we were wonky and cocked at an angle, twisting like a listing ship struggling to stay afloat and getting battered by the waves.

"With that module punctured—" Kal put her hand to her chin while her lips moved slightly. I could tell she was working the math. She tapped a few more keys, doing some sort of calculation, and then pointed to a new readout below the diagram.

26:31:14 and counting down.

"Twenty-six hours," Kal whispered. "That's how long until we completely lose orbit and reenter the atmosphere."

David snorted. "Except we wouldn't actually reenter. We'd be toasted marshmallows. S'mores, anyone?"

"Not funny!" Mae slugged him in the shoulder.

He pretended it hurt. "What?"

"The Zvezda," Kal said.

"You're right," Mae added. "The Russian service module could conduct a burn to alter the orbit of the ship. It's one method to conduct a debris avoidance maneuver."

"It could push us back into a stable orbit?" David asked.

"Zvezda thrusters have been damaged." The voice startled me. I'd forgotten Commander Horowitz could hear us. "However, the *Aether* might be able to right the ISS. But we have another problem we're working. Stand by."

Often, visiting spacecraft such as the old shuttle would use their thrusters to give the ISS a boost. The ISS is perpetually decaying in its orbit, so instead of burning precious fuel on board the ISS, if the shuttle is already docked, why not take advantage of the extra rocket power? The *Aether* could perform the same service. At least we might be able to stabilize it. Though—

"I'm not sure it could correct this wobble." Mae stole my thought.

"I found it!" Kal said. She seemed relieved, which struck me as odd once she revealed what she'd found.

"What is it?" I asked.

"The debris field." She paused, her lips moving again while she did more math. "It must have been this, which is coming around again in"—Kal ticked her head to the side as the calculator in her brain finished up—"one hundred seventy-two minutes."

"Are you sure of that?" David asked.

"Confirmed," Commander Horowitz said. "We just heard the same from Joint Space Operations."

I patted Kal on the back. She had beat Houston.

And she'd confirmed it wasn't sabotage. Right?

Kal spread two fingers on the screen, which zoomed out her close-up view of the cockeyed ISS to show a broader view that included Earth. She tapped a few commands into a terminal window, and a solid white line appeared behind the ISS, showing where it had already traveled in its orbit. A dotted white line projected its path forward. A red line traced a wider elliptical orbit that also circled Earth and showed a crossover with the white line. At the junction, a timer counted down.

171 minutes.

"Listen, I'm going to talk with the others, and with Houston," the commander said. "We'll come up with something. Signing off for now, but just ping us if you need us. Okay?"

"Roger that," Mae said, and we heard the comms click off.

Mae pointed at the screen in front of Kal. "That looks like it'll hit from behind and above the ISS. Is that right?"

"Yes." Kal tottered her head back and forth. "Which is good and bad."

"I fail to see the good here," David said. I agreed.

"NASA expects," Mae elaborated, "that most space debris will come head-on, which is why the forward-exposed pieces of the station are more heavily protected. The Whipple shield, for example, has several layers that obliterate and slow down micrometeorites. Those aren't totally uncommon, and the ISS has multiple spots of damage. Spacewalkers are even told to make sure to look where they grab in case a new micrometeorite has cranked up a sharp piece of metal that might tear their suit."

"Not helping," I said.

Mae chuckled. "Right. Anyway, the shield is on our front, but the debris field is coming from above and behind."

"That's the bad part," Kal added.

"*And* the good part." Mae shrugged.

I threw out my palms in a gesture of *How so?*

"Remember where the *Aether* is docked?" Mae answered, pausing for me to figure it out.

"Oh, I get it." The *Aether* was docked on the *forward* PMA-2 port, meaning our engines were the most forward part of the ISS, theoretically protecting the more sensitive cockpit from any debris that might hit from that direction. But if that barrage of debris had damaged our engines, we'd be stuck.

"Because the debris came from behind instead of from the front, the ISS acted as a giant shield for the *Aether*. That's probably why the Zvezda rockets in the aft were damaged," Kal said.

Mae nodded. "And this elliptical orbit of the debris,

and the fact it's coming from behind, means it's approaching slower, which buys us more time. If the debris were coming straight for us on a similar orbit as ours, we'd have a lot less than—" She pointed at the countdown timer. "One hundred sixty-eight minutes."

"But . . ." Kal trailed off, bringing up a new view on the monitor. "The bigger problem. I think I know what the commander has on his mind."

David threw his hands up. "The ISS dropping for early burnup, space junk about to collide with us and rip us to space dust—what could be the bigger problem?"

Kal pointed to the screen, which showed six blue bars on a chart. Two of them were full, but the other four were dropping rapidly. "This shows the oxygen supply on the ISS."

Watching them plummet, I found myself taking a deep, conscious breath. Echoing my thoughts, Mae asked, "How's ours?"

"The *Aether* is fine, miraculously. Thank the ISS for absorbing the brunt of that storm." Kal looked up with an almost guilty expression on her face, and I recognized it as concern for the adults left on the ISS.

We had plenty of oxygen.

They did not.

"They can electrolyze water to make oxygen," Mae said.

Kal shook her head and mouthed to us, *Not enough.*

"What do you mean?" David asked, desperation in his voice.

"I'm sure Houston is aware and working the problem," Kal said loudly, eyeing the intercom. But it was off, right? Could they still hear us?

"Don't give me that," David scoffed. He pushed to get closer to Kal, up in her face. "How long?"

Kal held firm, eyes locked with David's. She swallowed hard, then finally blinked and lowered her gaze back to the screen. "If my calculations are correct, then our parents won't have to worry about burning up with reentry or exploding from space junk. They'll run out of oxygen first."

Chapter 21

"I don't know, *exactly*." Kal finally got flustered with David's pressing questions about how much breathable oxygen was left on the ISS. "I told you, best I can guess is maybe two hours."

David floated away with his hand to his forehead and mumbled, "Two hours."

"There are two Soyuz escape capsules still attached to the ISS," Mae said. "Those can take three people each."

"If they're not damaged," Kal said.

"But there are eleven people over there." David pointed to the window. "If six left in the two Soyuz, that would still leave five of them on station."

"They'd let our parents go—and Fin's uncle—right?" Mae asked. But she looked down as soon as she said it. How could you choose something like that? Were any of their lives more important than the others'?

The fact was: if our four guardians took the capsules,

plus two of either the *Aether* or ISS crew, that would still doom five brave people to death.

"The ISS has four space suits, right?" I asked. "There's oxygen enough in those for hours." I thought it was a pretty good idea, given the circumstances.

"Yes, but that would still leave one person without," Kal answered. "Unless they traded off."

"I know," I said. "And the oxygen on the station would stretch longer if they weren't all breathing it."

She smiled at that, and her eyes got wide. "That's a great idea."

"Well, call 'em," Mae said. "It's worth a shot."

As Kal was reaching to hit the comms button, it flashed, and the commander's voice spoke from the speakers. "*Aether*, this is ISS. We have an idea."

"We do too," Kal said. "Actually, Fin does."

"Okay, great. Why don't you go first?"

I didn't expect the commander of the *Aether* to give me the floor, but I briefly recapped the idea to use the suits for their oxygen, thereby extending the supply on board.

"Excellent idea," he responded. "And it overlaps with what we're thinking. Commander Smith and Flight Engineer Morales are going to do an IVA."

That's an intravehicular activity, what NASA calls a space walk inside a vessel in a vacuum; it still requires a full suit and depressurization, but it's not technically outside the spaceship, which would be an EVA.

"What do you mean?" David asked.

"They're going to investigate the damage to the Harmony module. It seems like it was a sizable event so we can't guarantee our kit will have what we need to repair it, but we do have some patch capabilities. One of my buddies plugged a hole with his thumb once. Temporarily. Remind me to tell you that story later." The commander chuckled once, like he was remembering that day.

His lighthearted moment actually made me feel better. For a second.

When no one spoke, the commander continued, "Yes, well, this will necessitate that we first depressurize the connected Destiny module with the two spacewalkers inside, before they open the hatch to Harmony. You with me?"

"Affirmative," Mae responded.

"Good. So we just need you to hang tight while—"

"And if you don't repair it?" David asked.

"Well, son," the commander replied, "we have a backup plan for that contingency. Six of us will use the Soyuz capsules, and the remaining five will suit up and cross through the damaged module to the *Aether,* which will serve as the escape vehicle for the rest of us. Everyone will be safe."

"There's not enough time," Kal said. "Even if you

didn't have the oxygen leak, the debris will come around and hit us again in less than three hours. There are four EMUs and five of you, so you'd have to do multiple walks. To do all those decompressions and get everyone across . . . there's just not enough time." Her voice got quieter at the end. Then her face lit up. "What about the Chinese station, the Tiangong? Or that private one, the Genesis?"

"I like how you think," the commander said. "We contacted the Tiangong. They're aware of our situation and offered help, but they're too far away to do anything immediately. And they're rightly concerned about the debris as well. We didn't ask the Genesis for help since it's still early stages and doesn't have the capability to do any sort of rescue mission. Of course, they're watching us closely too."

"The whole world is probably watching," Mae added.

"Listen, kids. I'm not going to sugarcoat it," Commander Horowitz said. "This is a serious situation, so I need you to follow whatever orders you receive right away and without question. Just like we trained. Getting you kids detached and away from this crippled station is our top priority, and we're going to make that happen. One way or the other. You have my word. Do you understand me?"

"This plan is crazy!" David banged his fist against

the hull. "This is not happening." He yelled toward the radio, "Pappa? I will get a suit and come over there. Okay?" He shook. He moved toward the *Aether* air lock where we stored the EMUs.

"David," I said. "Just wait. You're not invincible. We have to do this as a team, or we'll fall apart. Just hold on." He pushed my arm away. "David, wait."

He turned on me. "This is not a game, Fin. My pappa, your uncle, the crew—they will die unless we do something."

"Your dad is in good hands. They're *astronauts*. They trained for years for these sorts of emergencies. You heard how calm Commander Horowitz sounded. And Houston has the best engineering minds on the planet figuring it out. 'Working the problem,' right? There's no way they're going to die."

David grasped me by the shoulders. "You don't get it, Fin. If they die—"

"They're not going to—"

"If they die, we all die."

Chapter 22

I floated to a window and stared out at the ISS. Shrapnel from the impact spun and glittered in the sunlight. There was more of it than I'd expected, and my hopes waned that they might be able to complete a full repair. Were they saying that they could fix the station just to lift our morale? Another one of those little lies?

Like when Dad had echoed what Mom said in the hospital, that everything would be all right. When, clearly, it wasn't.

David was right. If the adults couldn't get back to the *Aether*, we'd be stranded. Connected to a sinking ship, we'd go down too. Or even if we detached, then what?

The ISS listed at an odd angle to the horizon, definitely not in the attitude it had been when we first docked.

Something Commander Horowitz had said stuck

with me. He said *one way or the other*, their priority was to get us away from the crippled station. What did he mean by that? Even if it meant we didn't have them on board when we left? I mean, maybe only four of them could cross over in time to leave with us on the *Aether*. That would leave one unfortunate soul behind. Who would sacrifice themselves like that?

Would it be one of the ISS crew? Maybe Commander Smith had already volunteered to go down with her ship? Would they draw straws? I read about how the shipwrecked survivors from the whaling ship *Essex*, with diminishing supplies, drew straws to determine who would die first so the others might live . . .

It was unbearable to consider and put a lump in my throat. I looked away, back at my friends. They were floating quietly in the stuffy air, the severity of the situation overwhelming us.

Then things got worse.

Another Klaxon alarm bell sounded. An automated voice informed us, "Warning. Fire in Harmony module. Warning. Fire in—"

But Harmony was the already-damaged ISS module. The node that Commander Smith and Engineer Morales were currently inside, inspecting the damage, right? And how could a fire start in that vacuum? Wait, if a fire was able to start in there, did that mean it wasn't completely lost yet? Conflicting feelings of hope and fear warred inside me.

I pulled myself back to the window I'd floated away from, right as a concussion ripped the Harmony node open like a busted soda can. The blast tore a crack in the forward dome at the junction with the PMA-2 docking port that held the *Aether* to the station.

The fierce shock wave rattled our ship, sending reverberations through the metal frame, eliciting a yelp of surprise from several of us. I flopped around. Outside, I saw debris scattering in every direction. I scanned our cockpit with wide eyes and shallow breaths, waiting for the inevitable pop and whoosh of air evacuating into the void and—

"What happened?!" David shouted, and pushed himself to the window.

Kal held her hand like a wounded paw. I slid over to her and saw her wrist was already swollen.

"I'm fine," she said. "Banged it. Pretty hard."

"It looks sprained, or broken," I said.

"I'm fine," she insisted. But her chin trembled.

"Oh my god," David muttered. I wondered if he saw Commander Smith or Engineer Morales, floating away, lifeless.

"*Aether*, report." It was Commander Horowitz again, eerily calm. "You okay over there?"

Mae forced a breath to regain her composure, then responded in a similarly calm way. "Minor injuries, but we're okay. No alarms on the *Aether*. Sir, what was that?"

"Looks like we lost Harmony."

No kidding.

What about the crew? "Smith and Morales?" I asked.

"They're fine," the commander answered. "They were still depressurizing in Destiny, thankfully. But listen, the *Aether* is still docked with the PMA-2, which is now dangling from the wall of Harmony. So we want you to get clear of that damage, to avoid the *Aether* from taking any more lumps. Okay?"

"Uh, okay. Sir." Mae hesitated.

"Houston is going to walk you through what they're doing, but the maneuver will be remotely controlled from the ground. You'll just want to strap in and let them do their jobs. Affirmative?"

Wait, we were undocking from the ISS? And mission control could fly us remotely?

"We will *not* leave you behind," David yelled into the intercom. Kal nodded, still clutching her wrist close to her body.

"Top priority is to get you and the *Aether* clear of the ISS, pronto," Commander Horowitz said. "We can worry about what's next after that. But I don't plan on you leaving without my ride."

Kal tipped her head to get our attention, then pointed to the oxygen readout on her screen. Four of the tanks were now empty and offline. The other two tanks were more than half empty.

It was worse than before.

Whatever we were going to do, it had to be fast.

Chapter 23

Houston's countdown for undocking—"Three . . . two . . . one . . . and undocking initiated"—was immediately followed by a loud, crunching, scraping sound that did not sound nominal.

Then a high-pitched creaking and it stopped.

"*Aether*, this is Houston. We're gonna need someone to go up into the nose and give the docking mechanism a jiggle."

We exchanged confused glances.

"Sorry, Houston," Mae replied. "Did you say, 'a jiggle'?"

I snorted. *Jiggle* must be a technical term.

"That's correct, *Aether*. Systems report the docking mechanism is jammed, so we'd like you to give a twist on the manual override to see if you can dislodge it from inside."

I unbuckled my harness and pushed off toward the nose. David was right behind me.

Even with both hands on the manual override handle, I couldn't get it to budge. It was made more challenging because I wasn't anchored to anything to push against. I planted both feet and heaved, but nothing.

"Move aside, skinny," David said.

I moved aside.

David's arms were a lot thicker than mine, but he still needed something to counteract his twisting, so I wedged myself between the wall and David's side so he could lean on me to provide a backstop.

He heaved and . . . nothing.

"*Aether*, Houston. How's it going up there?"

"We're trying," Mae said. Then, to David, "Need some help?" She smirked.

David gave her a look, then rubbed his hands together and gripped the override handle fist over fist. I imagined it was how he grabbed hold of the gymnastic bars, like nothing could separate it from his body.

He heaved again and this time . . . *clunk*.

"*Aether*, Houston. We see that manual override was successful and the *Aether* has undocked."

"Yes!" I fist pumped. But immediately realized that meant we were now adrift.

"But, uh, *Aether*, can you give us a reading on your remote-connection status?"

Mae looked to Kal, who tapped around on the screen with her one uninjured hand.

We all saw it, flashing in red:

REMOTE HOUSTON CONTROL: DISCONNECTED

"Houston? It says we're disconnected," Mae reported.

"Confirmed, *Aether*. Stand by."

"Stand by? Houston, we're drifting here. What do you mean 'stand by'?"

"We're working the problem, *Aether*. Stand by."

The comms switched off.

We were floating freely. Out the window, I could see the damaged PMA-2 docking port. A huge piece of metal stuck out like a spear, mere centimeters from where our hatch had connected. That must have been what fouled up our separation. If it had pierced any closer, it would have punctured straight into our ship, and we'd have been goners.

"Guys," I said. I was pretty sure the color had evaporated from my face. "Look."

A piece of very jagged shrapnel was rotating like a circular saw and spinning right toward us. It was moving at a pace that told me we had maybe a minute until impact.

"Shoot. I'm gonna get us outta here," Mae said. She pulled down the two joysticks for manual control on armrest-like foldouts.

I stared, dumbfounded. David tapped me on the back as he floated past toward his jump seat. "Better strap in."

"Ten of twelve thruster quads for the reaction control system are online." Kal tapped around on her screen. "Two forward nodes not reporting."

"It'll have to do," Mae said. She exhaled and gripped the joysticks.

"I'm trying to reboot—whoa!" Kal jolted sideways.

I hadn't even finished buckling when Mae hit the controls. We heard the *pshhhhh* of compressed propellant shooting from the thrusters and felt the sudden delta-vee of movement. I gripped my armrests so tightly I thought I might rip them off.

Mae had done awesome in the simulators, I told myself. I mean, I'm pretty great at video games too, but this! This was no game. I thought back to what David had said about "This is not a game" and everyone dying.

Psh psh psh.

But Mae was actually piloting the *Aether*. In space. For real. Pretty freaking amazing. "You're doing it, Mae!"

"Of course I am," she replied coolly. "Almost clear. Just a few more—"

Just then something toward the aft of our ship scraped hard and made me wince.

"Damage report." Mae looked over at Kal.

"I—I don't—" Kal stuttered, staring at the screen.

Sweat dotted my forehead.

"Damage report!" Mae shouted.

It snapped Kal awake. "No alarms." Her face squished up in confusion. "The debris, the explosion—and the system is reporting no major damage. That can't be right, can it? I'm going to run another diagnostic on the software itself. I wonder if it got fried or something."

"A lucky break?" I said.

"Maybe." David's eyes were locked on the ISS out the window, floating farther away from us now. "But we're not out of this yet. Our parents and the astronauts are still on that station."

The ISS jittered and seized like a zombie insect, all cockeyed. Sparks spit into the dark and winked out like fireflies. I think our clunky undocking might have added to its funky wobble. Seeing it in such a decrepit state, knocked from its normally majestic perch, that brief feeling that we were fortunate for making it this far came crashing down, like I knew the ISS was fated to do.

"How long 'til the debris hits?" I asked. No answer. "Kal?"

Her eyes flitted across the screen.

"Kal?"

"Shh, hold on." She waved at me dismissively.

I couldn't do anything but stare at the ISS in its death dance.

"*Aether*, this is Houston. We saw the whole thing. Great job, Mae."

Everyone smiled at Mae. David clapped.

"Bad news is," Houston continued, "we have not been able to reestablish the remote control link. Good news is, you have a heck of a pilot there. We want you to increase your trajectory to the orbit we're sending now; then you'll hold that position and stand by for a pickup. It might be a little while, but we're already prepping a rescue rocket to come up there and get you. Okay?"

"Roger that, Houston. But why can't we just reenter?" Mae asked.

"We considered that risk, *Aether*. Given the fireworks up there, we're concerned your heat shield might have sustained some damage."

He didn't have to finish the thought. Though the space shuttle program ran for thirty years and had 135 successful missions, two of those were total-loss disasters. The first seven crew members died in the *Challenger* explosion forty years ago, in 1986. And the second seven, which came to our minds now, were lost when the space shuttle *Columbia* tried to reenter in 2003. During launch, a piece of foam had broken off from the big external tank and dinged a hole in the heat shield on *Columbia's* wing. The crew made it safely to space and did their work, but upon reentry that hole in the wing ripped apart their craft and killed all seven crew members.

If the *Aether* had any damage to its heat shield, we could become another mortality statistic. And I certainly didn't want to skew the numbers in the wrong direction.

I nodded at Mae.

"Roger that, Houston. Standing by." She sounded quieter than usual, waited a second more, and then flipped off the comms.

Kal undid her belt and flew up to the window, her hand on the pane and her face so close it fogged the glass. I knew she was thinking about her father on the ISS. "They're not going to make it."

I slid up next to her. "Don't say that. They'll make it."

She shook her head. The moisture stuck to her eyes and jiggled back and forth. Due to the surface tension, tears didn't float free like in the movies. The water clung to her skin, and she had to wipe it away with her sleeve. She sniffled.

"I was calculating the debris orbit when Houston called," she said. "I think the reason they wanted us to increase our orbit is because the debris field has spread. Maybe it collided with a satellite or something. It's coming around again sooner than I last predicted, and it's bigger this time, moving faster. The debris field is going to hit again *before* they run out of oxygen. Getting them into the suits won't matter."

"But NASA is sending a rescue ship . . ." I trailed off because I knew there was no way they could prep and launch a ship in time.

Uncle D was on that station. I brought him because he was my wild funcle and I didn't have to worry about feelings with him like I did every time I looked at my mom and dad since the accident. And now here I was, having to worry about him too. It made me angry.

"We'll be saved by that rocket," I said. I had to believe it. The alternative was too terrible. I wouldn't accept it.

Kal scrunched her eyelids tightly. Apparently, she'd built up so many tears that some of her salt water actually broke free and bobbled toward the window. "Maybe we'll make it, Fin. But everyone on the ISS is doomed."

Chapter 24

David smacked his hand on the side of the *Aether* hull so hard I flinched, worried for a second he might punch right through. "Easy, buddy," I said, palms out.

"We can't just sit here and watch them die!" The veins in his neck bulged and his face pulsed red.

"We'll fix this," I said.

"How, Fin? How?!"

I pointed to the ISS. No one could tell specifically what I was pointing at because of the distance, but I was trying to draw attention to the still-intact PMA-3 docking port on the zenith of Harmony. The forward portion of the module had blown open, but the rest of the tube still looked relatively intact. No pressure, obviously, but—

"We can dock to PMA-3," I said, simply, trying to appear calm despite the boiling emotions inside. It was like I was competing, even now, showing I could stay in control more than David. I could fake it, and they'd think I had my stuff together.

Mae let out a deep sigh. "The station is too erratic, up and down and sideways. There's no way we could match it to get a decent docking connection."

"But we can try, right?" My face was hot now. I thought the leather-jacket-wearing, daredevil Mae would agree with me on this.

Mae moved her head slightly back and forth, back and forth, seeming to consider it. "No way. It's impossible."

I pushed off the wall next to David and careened over to Mae. "Come on, pilot." I said it with snark, challenging her. "You can do this."

She bristled and narrowed her eyes. "You don't think I want to save them, Fin? My stepmom is on that station too, you know! And though we've had our differences, I don't want her to die."

"What about one of the other docking ports on the Russian segments?" Kal asked.

Mae turned to face Kal, seemingly happy to give me her back. "The Soyuz capsules are berthed there, but even if they weren't, the docking mechanisms are different. We couldn't connect there with the *Aether* even in normal circumstances."

David scooted in behind me and hit the switch for the comms. "Houston, is there any other way to save them? No rescue rocket will get here in time. So, what can we do? There must be—"

"*Aether*, this is Houston. We can discuss this once you've raised your orbit to a safe distance away from the next orbital conjunction. We don't have time to—"

"No!" David smashed his fist on the panel. "We have to save them. I will not lose my pappa. He . . . He's all I have now."

David's rage and sorrow were contagious. There had to be something we could do. NASA has the smartest engineers in the world. We didn't just leave astronauts to die.

"David, son." It was his dad, over the radio. "Do what Houston commands. Raise orbit. Is all right, son. All right. You be safe. Is what Mom would want too."

"Mom doesn't care about us," David snapped. "I won't leave you like she left us."

"Of course she cares, son. She probably watching right now."

David swallowed and looked around, apparently realizing everyone was watching him. "There must be something we can do."

"I know, I know," his dad said. "I want to be with you too. Very bad. But you have to do what astronauts command. Is all right."

There was that lie again.

"No, it's not," David replied.

His dad laughed. "Well, is true, but you need to ride

this like you do on motocross. What is you say?"

"What?" David looked confused, like he was thinking, *How could he compare this to dirt bikes?*

"Keep eyes on jump in front of you," his dad said.

David hung his head, then rubbed his face.

"*Aether*, this is Commander Horowitz. We don't have much more time. Your parents are going to be safe. You have my word. We have two perfectly capable Soyuz escape capsules, if it comes to that. Your parents don't want to leave you any more than you want to leave them. But the reality of our situation is that we might have to split up in order to save everyone. Now please do as Houston says and burn into the safe orbit."

A second of silence, as we were all speechless. I was numb.

"*Aether*, Houston. Initiate burn procedure immediately." That calm voice again. How could they be so calm? If *their* lives were on the line, would they be so calm then?

"Roger that, Houston." Mae sounded almost as copacetic. "Strap in." She gestured with her head toward our seats, indicating we should buckle up.

I went through the motions, my feelings turned off.

Psh psh psh psssshhhhh. Mae was a smooth operator.

"Uh, *Aether*, this is Houston."

Hm, maybe they have good news for us this time?

"I'm sorry, but we're gonna need you to abort the

planned burn. Repeat, abort the burn."

Mae put her hands up in the air, and the thrusters quit.

Already? We just started!

"Thank you, *Aether*. Now please move immediately to the magnetic shelter on board. We received an alert from NOAA. They've detected an unexpected solar flare and a large CME. With everything going on, we didn't see the warning earlier, so we predict less than five minutes before the first particles hit the *Aether*. But that's plenty of time to move down into the safety of the shelter, where you'll be protected from the radiation. Acknowledge?"

For a second, we looked at one another and processed what we'd just heard. NOAA is the National Oceanic and Atmospheric Administration. They run the Space Weather Prediction Center, which monitors for sun events like solar flares and coronal mass ejections (CMEs), which are basically like giant explosions in the sun that belch radioactive material in the form of protons, as well as magnetic energy that can cause temporary blackouts in navigation and communications signals. Those bursts hitting Earth's protective magnetic field give us the beautiful auroras, the northern lights.

Solar flares happen relatively regularly, but this CME must have been an extra big anomaly, big enough to pose a real problem. If we didn't get to our magnetic shelter lower down in the ship, we would get a toxic dose of radiation. It could hurt us like a thousand dental X-rays if we were unprotected during the bombardment.

Definitely not good news.

"Acknowledged," Mae said. "Let's go." She was the first to unbuckle her harness. We followed suit and rushed down to the magnetic shelter, which is also the exercise room on the *Aether*. Its walls are lined with water between two layers to absorb the radiation and a magnetic field to shield us from the energetic particles.

We get the beautiful auroras when the radiation hits our planet, but that beauty is really Earth's magnetic field protecting life from the harmful blasts. Scientists think maybe Mars used to have a magnetic field that enabled life to grow there, but when it lost the field, the sun baked off the oceans and killed all living things.

So, yeah, good to have a magnetic force field between us and the barrage about to hammer through our ship.

We passed the *Aether* air lock and descended to the exercise room, aka the radiation shelter.

David hit the bike, no doubt working off some nervous frustration. Kal floated near a window with her arms folded across her chest. I thought about going over to her, about asking her why she'd been acting odd on the ISS before it blew up, but she seemed to want some alone time right now. And I didn't know how to ask such a question. I was curious, but it felt more like an accusation. And I didn't want to start a fight among all our other challenges. And truly, what did it matter anymore? We had bigger problems.

"*Aether*, Houston. Can you confirm you're in the shelter?"

"We are, Houston," I said. "How long do you think this storm will last?"

"Looks like it'll be a very brief one, fortunately. Not certain, but could be half an hour, plus or minus. Keep an eye on your readout, and it'll tell you when it's safe to return to the cockpit."

"Understood, Houston."

"Looks like it should be hitting us any minute," Mae reported, watching the screen's predicted visualization of the ionized energy approaching our ship.

"*Aether*, Houston. After—going—we're—" The static increased.

"We lost comms," Kal said.

"Temporarily, right?" David asked.

Kal shrugged. "Probably."

"Probably?" David stopped biking. "You mean you don't know?"

"No, David. I don't," Kal snapped.

"Sorry," David said. "It's not your fault."

"Of course not," Mae said.

Kal said nothing, just pulled her knees up to her chest and buried her head in the crook of her arm. She hung there like a ball, one of her dyed purple strands of hair sticking straight out like she was suspended on a string, like one little snip of that thread and she'd fall apart.

I think we all felt that delicate right now. But I wasn't ready to admit it out loud.

Chapter 25

About twenty minutes later, the radiation detector on the monitor turned to green, indicating the solar storm had passed. David jokingly complained about such a short workout as we filed back up into the cockpit.

I looked out the window, afraid at what I might find left of the ISS.

"Houston, ISS, this is *Aether*, come in," Mae said into the intercom.

No answer.

"Houston, ISS, this is the *Aether*. You there?"

No answer.

"Houston, ISS, anyone. This is the starship *Aether*. Please come in."

Mae tried three more times. All with no answer.

"Why aren't the comms up?" David asked, frustrated.

Kal tapped away at the keyboard. "I thought they'd come back online after the radiation passed, but they're still down. Systems are a little off, things not reporting right, and . . ." She put her finger to her chin.

"And what?" I asked.

"I don't know," she said. "I think that solar storm may have fried some of our circuits. Our comms could be down permanently."

Mae exhaled heavily. *Ugh.*

She was right. Could anything else go wrong? In hindsight, I shouldn't have tempted fate. But at the time, I chuckled.

"What's so funny?" David asked.

"Kal, you know what an astronaut's favorite key is on the keyboard?" I asked.

"What?" David asked. He didn't sound curious about the answer, only confused about why I was even asking such a silly question.

Kal didn't miss a beat. Without looking up, she answered the joke. "The space bar."

I laughed. I mean, it was a terrible joke. But also kinda funny. Astronaut's favorite key is the space bar? "Okay, here's another one. Why didn't the restaurant on the Moon do well?"

David hadn't stopped staring at me, mouth slightly open, and Mae joined him, looking like I'd lost it. I told you; I tend to make jokes when I'm nervous. "So, you give up?"

Kal didn't look up from her keyboard while she

deadpanned: "Because it didn't have any atmosphere."

"Oh! She nailed it, ladies and gentlemen!" I laughed and spun in a circle. "I'm here all week!"

"Maybe longer," Mae said. Okay, that was NOT funny.

My first out-of-this-world standup routine was rudely interrupted by yet another warning indicator. This one about the incoming debris field.

"But we're out of range of that, right?" David asked.

"We aborted the avoidance burn," Mae said, strapping into her harness. "We need to get out of here, quick."

"The ISS is gonna get hit." David said it as a matter of fact, not as an argument.

"Initiating burn in three . . . two . . . one." Mae hit the joysticks, and the subtle delta-vee pushed me into my seat.

Kal whispered something.

"What?" I asked.

"I found something," Kal said, pointing to her screen. "We can do it."

"Found what?" David asked.

"I found the reentry procedure," Kal said. "I could walk Mae through it."

I peered out the window at the station, getting farther away. Terrible daydreams flashed in my mind before I could shut them out: of the adults inside suffocating, or getting pummeled by supersonic bullets of debris, or burning up with atmospheric reentry, screaming that we'd left them behind. Terrible, scary images.

No. I shook my head and squeezed my eyes shut, hands on my temples. *No!*

We couldn't abandon them.

"Look!" David shouted.

When I opened my eyes, I saw David pointing out the window.

The Soyuz capsules, both of them, had separated from the station.

"I guess that means our parents are reentering," Kal said.

"*If* our parents are on those boats." David unbuckled and floated closer to the window, blocking my view.

They would have put our parents on those escape pods first, right? Just like Commander Horowitz had said? But we didn't have any way of confirming with our comms down.

Since both Soyuz capsules had departed, that meant six adults were currently on their way to a hard landing in the desert of Kazakhstan. Or maybe a watery splashdown somewhere in the Atlantic.

It also meant there were still five adults left on the ISS.

"ISS, this is the *Aether*, come in . . . ISS, this is *Aether*, come in . . . Houston, *Aether*, come in . . . " Mae tried over and over again.

I let out a breath and inhaled again, deep into my lungs. I hoped, and kind of had to assume, that Uncle D was on one of those Soyuz. But I also thought about the five astronauts left on board the ISS. If they'd sent our four guardians, they could have also sent either two of the ISS crew or two of the *Aether* crew. Was Christa, our smiling tour guide, on her way home right now? Or still stuck on a doomed ship?

As I contemplated this, the sun disappeared over the horizon, plunging us back into darkness.

We floated silently. No comms. No time. No options.

I spoke, but quietly. "I was up all night wondering where the sun had gone. Then, it dawned on me . . ."

No one laughed.

Chapter 26

"We can't just leave them," Kal said. "All systems on the *Aether* are nominal, so we have—"

"Besides the comms," David interrupted. "Look, I don't want to leave them either. But our parents were very likely in those Soyuz escape vehicles. We need to get out of here and reenter. It's obviously what's best if the Soyuz capsules left too. They're abandoning ship. They know it's the last chance we have."

"The ISS still has some probability of recovery," Kal said, shaking her head. "It took some damage, yes, but it can be repaired. If we can get to it before the debris does."

"That's a pretty dangerous game of chicken," David said, pointing to the readout showing the elliptical orbit of the debris field and its position approaching us rapidly.

"You guys, we can't just reenter," I said. "Remember the *Columbia*? We need to wait it out up here until we can get help to inspect our heat shield. Like it or not, we're stuck."

"Our life support shows nominal," Kal reported. "We're using more oxygen than normal, but there aren't as many of us here now as was planned for. So, we have plenty of air."

"I have an idea," Mae said. "We nudge the ISS, gently, like a tugboat, and push it out of the orbit of the debris to somewhere safe. That would at least buy them some more time."

"That's an awfully huge gamble," David said, shaking his head.

"Aren't you the big, bad motocross biker who puts his life on the line for kicks?" Mae teased.

David narrowed his eyes at her, but with a faint grin. "Fine." He threw up his arms. "Fine. Do it. Crash into that hulking wreck with our delicate ship and hope we don't all die together. I take risks, but this would not be a risk. It would be foolish."

Half-dazed, I watched the ISS wobbling on its axis and imagined it in flames like the jet engine from my dreams where I'm flying at Mach 1. The dream where I end up paralyzed at the end.

Eject! Eject!

Wait. That's it! Maybe.

"I have an idea," I mumble.

"Is it any saner than ramming the International

Space Station?" David scoffed. Mae scowled at him.

"Well," I said, "hear me out before you decide that."

I hesitated. It was definitely a wild idea.

"Come on, Fin. What is it?" Kal asked.

She blinked her big eyes, and I couldn't help but blurt it out. "Maybe the astronauts on the ISS could eject."

"Eject?" David asked. "Oh, wow, this is—this is getting ridiculous. The only thing to do is—"

"Hear him out," Kal interrupted forcefully. Her tone surprised me. And her support emboldened me.

"Besides my custom EMU, we have two other space suits on the *Aether*." I was talking directly to Kal. "Two of us could wait right outside the *Aether* air lock, tethered to our ship. The adults could jump from the ISS out the Quest air lock over to us. We'd catch them."

I looked at my hands, then back to Kal, then over to David and Mae. I was shocked that David hadn't shot the idea down right away. Nor was he laughing.

But then he smiled. "Catch 'em like a rugby ball." He thumped my shoulder with his fist. "Sounds safer than ramming them."

"I'll go out with David," Mae said. "And I'll use Fin's SAFER prototype. I'm a pilot. If anyone goes off course in their jump, I could scoot out and bring them back safely to the *Aether*."

"Yeah, you're the pilot. That's why we need you in

here," I said. "In case . . . I don't know. In case."

"Makes sense to me, Mae. You should stay on the ship to fly us around," David said. "And Kal has a busted wrist. So, that means—looks like it's you and me, Fin."

"That's it?" I asked, shocked at David's sudden change in stance. "Five seconds ago, you wanted to cut and run and reenter. Now you want to do this super dangerous thing?"

David looked slightly offended by my choice of words. "Fin, come on. I don't want to leave them, but I had no idea how we could help. Your plan could work. And if it doesn't . . ." He didn't finish his sentence.

"What?" I asked.

"If it doesn't work," Kal stepped in, "then we're no worse off than we are now. You both come back into the *Aether*. And we wait, alone."

"Except we're putting ourselves into harm's way with the debris coming around," I pointed out.

"Speaking of that, if we're gonna do this we better hurry," Mae said. "Strap yourselves in, and I'll boost us closer."

"Wait," Kal said. "There are only four space suits on the ISS."

Four space suits and five adults. We're still one short.

"And comms are down," she added. "How are we going to tell them this plan? They'll have to know to jump to us."

I realized what I had to do. It was crystal clear. "I'll go. Alone. I'll jump."

"What, like one giant leap?" Mae smirked. I recognized Neil Armstrong's famous words from when he'd first stepped onto the surface of the Moon back in 1969.

Like his, this would be the biggest jump of my life.

"I'll take an extra space suit from the *Aether* attached to my back," I said. "The extra suit, plus the four they have on the ISS, will be enough for everyone to have an EMU." I ran through it in my head. "I'll get to the ISS, knock on the air lock, and get them to open up."

This time David bust out laughing while flashing the *hang loose* sign. "Wow, Fin, you ARE crazy! Awesome!" He put up his fist for a bump.

"No way," Kal said. "That is much too high a risk."

"It'll be fiiiiine," I said, in a silly, happy-go-lucky way. "I'll tether myself to the *Aether*. If anything goes wrong, I'll just rewind myself back in."

"The tethers are 85 feet long, but—" Mae pointed to a busted radiator array blocking our path. "There's no way I could fly the *Aether* within 85 feet of the Quest air lock without us getting clobbered."

She was right. The crinkled component stuck out at an awkward angle that would smash into us if we got close enough for a tether to make it across.

"I'll use multiple tethers, then." I shrugged.

"I want to go," David said. "Sounds fun."

"Just keep your eyes on the jump in front of you," I said.

"That's right." David nodded with a grin.

Mae shook her head. "I still think I should be the one doing it. I'm the pilot."

David, Mae, and I devolved into a near shouting match talking over one another.

"Wait!" Kal shouted. That got our attention. "I went on vacation in Sri Lanka once. And took a zip-line ride."

She let it hang in the air. It took me a second, but I thought I understood what she was getting at. "A zip line from the *Aether* to the ISS? Using the tethers."

Kal didn't acknowledge. Instead, she was looking out the window, probably calculating the distance.

"How do we get the line across?" Mae said. "We still need someone to fly it over there."

"We could tie two tethers together, then secure it to the handhold on the outside of Quest," Kal said.

I liked the idea. I pushed myself down to the *Aether* air lock area, searching for two of the retractable metal cables used as tethers. "And the adults could hand-over-hand shimmy across from the ISS to the *Aether*, while still being attached to the lifeline." I pulled a piece of the cable taut between my two fists.

Mae laughed. "Ziiiiip liiiine iiiinnn spppaaaaaace!" She splayed her hands like she was pitching a movie.

"This is a plan," Kal said. "Is there a better one?"

"Note that she didn't say it's a *good* plan," David joked.

"It's our only plan," I said, pulling my folded liquid-ventilation garment from the Velcro securing it to the wall above my space suit. "We can't toss the line over. They'd never know it was us. They'd probably just think it was space junk plinking on the hull. We have to—*I* have to—fly over there and knock."

"And hope they answer," Mae said.

"Their oxygen is low," Kal said. I think she was implying that they might not be responsive. Maybe they were unconscious. Then she added, "But they should still be alive. We have to hurry."

"Get us over there!" I shouted up to Mae.

"Roger that. Hold on." Mae fired up the thrusters.

David worked his way down to me at the air lock, holding onto things to prevent the acceleration from throwing him off.

"Did you think I'm going to let you win this one so easy, Fin?"

"Win?"

David held up his fist in his palm. I knew what that meant. He wanted to asteroid-moon-planet for it. "Winner takes the space walk and becomes the hero."

First round, my asteroid beat his planet.

Second round, we both drew planet.

Third round, we both drew planet.

"Is this really necessary?" Mae asked. "You're wasting time."

"Oh, this is very necessary," David said.

He threw a crescent moon but instantly groaned and threw his hands in the air when he saw that I'd dropped another planet. Another clean sweep, 2–0.

"Man, how do you do that every time?" He looked in my eyes like he couldn't believe it. "Fine, I get to do the space walk next time, then."

I laughed at that. "Hopefully, there won't be a next time."

"Just don't pee in the suit, okay?"

"I'll save the barf bag for you."

David laughed at that but mimicked a punch in my direction, with a smile.

The liquid-cooled ventilation garment is like a onesie pair of long johns with tubes all over it. Water flows through the tubes and is then exposed to the freezing temperatures of space within your backpack life-support system to cool it down, then circulated over your entire body to keep you from overheating, since the sun is blasting you up to hundreds of degrees Fahrenheit. And there are heating units to take the chill out when the sun disappears and plunges the temperature a few hundred degrees in the opposite direction.

It's useful, but certainly not meant to be fashionable. All that is to say, I felt pretty awkward in the tubed pajamas and hurried to the next step of getting into the EMU.

As David helped me into the legs of the space suit, I noticed Kal had a wire snaking from my SAFER prototype into the laptop Velcroed to her thigh. With her uninjured hand, she was pecking out keystrokes in a hurry.

"What are you doing?" I asked.

"Almost done." Then she unplugged the cable and floated over to us, guiding the boxy SAFER in front of her.

"It was going to be a surprise," she said. "I wrote a little software mod for your unit. AAH, for Automatic Attitude Hold. It's not quite done yet, and I thought we could play with it on the test firings in the *Aether* on the trip to the Moon. It's really just beta software and hasn't had any QA testing, and I think I got most of the big bugs, but—I'm sure it'll be fine. Probably."

"Uh," I stammered. "Thanks?"

"What's Automatic Attitude Hold do?" David asked, pushing the suit's upper half over my arms. "Fin's attitude seems all right."

I rolled my eyes, but I heard Mae chuckle. "Don't

encourage him, Mae!"

Kal ignored the banter. "If you get into a spin—like, an uncontrollable spin—this red light should flash. You just flip this switch here on your control stick, and the AAH software will take over. It'll automatically adjust your pitch, yaw, and roll to get you back into a stable position in x, y, z space."

"Sorta like an autopilot," I said.

"Well, it won't take you anywhere," she answered. "But if you start wobbling and can't recover, the AAH should do its job to stop you."

I noticed her use of the word *should*. "That's awesome. Thank you, Kal."

She smiled and looked away.

David brought the helmet down over my head and sealed out the sound of the cabin. Then I could feel him securing the SAFER onto my backpack.

"Comms check," I said.

Mae shook her head. I read her lips, and I'm pretty sure she said, "No dice."

Great, no comms here either.

I'd be flying truly solo.

Chapter 27

I stepped into the *Aether* decompression chamber and spun the dial to evacuate the atmosphere into space. David and Kal watched from the tiny porthole window.

The readout dropped down to zero, an alert tone chimed, and a light turned from green to red. I was free to open the hatch into space. But was I ready?

Couldn't very well decide against it now, could I?

The door latch twisted easily, and before I knew it, I'd pushed the hatch open and was staring straight out into the void of space. Mae had maneuvered the *Aether* underneath the station, so I was looking straight up at the Quest air lock above me. I knew that below me, Earth was spinning past.

I reached out and anchored my cabling tether to a recessed clip on the external wall of the hull. I gave it a tug. Then another. I could feel David and Kal watching me from behind. The extra space suit was clipped to my back, and as I put my head out the hatch, I could feel it bump into the opening. Oops.

I moved the extra suit down beneath my feet so I could fit through the exit. It took a lot more physical effort and jostling than I thought it should to get myself and the extra suit out of the air lock. I didn't really have a chance to look around, trying to get my clunky suit and the one attached to me out of the air lock as gracefully as possible, which wasn't very graceful. I could imagine the jokes David would be cracking if the comms weren't busted, and I had to chuckle at the comic absurdity of the moment.

Once I was fully outside of the *Aether*, I paused to catch my breath, grasping a handhold to steady myself. I panted heavily and could feel my heart pounding in my ears. Inside the suit was almost as noisy as the ISS, the constant hum of a fan circulating my oxygen. But that sound meant my systems were working as they should, so it was a welcome buzzing.

That was when I finally had a moment to look around, and it freaked me out. I tightened my grip on the handhold, but it felt much too small. Looking down at Earth, my brain was trying to tell me that I was falling, or that I was going to fall, or that I should be falling. It was odd.

I closed my eyes and reminded my brain I was able to hang there, effortlessly, safely.

I took a few deep breaths. I could do this.

When I opened my eyes again, Earth still looked like a long, long drop away, but I didn't get that same sense of vertigo. I looked up and away from Earth. The ISS was a lot farther away than it had seemed from within the safe confines of the *Aether*. I knew it was a trick of my imagination, but I also wondered what the heck I'd been thinking to volunteer for this dangerous mission.

Not to say I wanted to go inside quite yet. I'd been dreaming of doing an EVA, a real live space walk. In space! For real! And here I was. Doing it. Floating in the vacuum.

Okay, I was still gripping that handhold too tight. I could feel sweat on my palm. I knew I'd have to let go sooner or later. Which made me remember the countdown timer of that debris field. If I didn't move quickly, we'd all be getting a visit from space-junk cannon fire.

I couldn't overthink it anymore; I had to just go. I had to just—push.

And I did.

I was floating away from the *Aether*.

I could feel the subtle whir of the tether uncoiling. It counteracted the force of my push, and I was slowing down gently, so I engaged the SAFER for the first time. It occurred to me, obviously too late: Why hadn't I tested it inside first? No time, I rationalized. No time to be dawdling out here either. I had to move.

I couldn't hear the propellant blasts, but I could most definitely feel them. The thrusters pushed the SAFER into my back, and I started moving forward, but not in a direct line to the Quest. I knew I had to conserve my fuel, so no time for joyriding or detours. I flicked the controls to adjust my pitch, then yaw, talking to myself out loud through the whole thing. I tried to imagine that I was simply in the simulator again. No big deal.

"Little bump there and oops, too much. That's okay. Little bit on the other side and—dang it." I let go of the controls. I was making it worse. "Cool, cool, cool, it's cool. Gentle on the controls, you got this."

I echoed that to myself again: "You got this." But each time I repeated it, I wondered if I really was going to make it or if I was in over my head. My tether stretched, and I started to roll a little. It would be one thing if I was flying without the cable pulling on me, but with that tension, ever so slight, I had to counter that force. It was difficult, like dividing fractions while trying to land a plane sideways. None of the simulators had trained me for this.

Then a loud *BEEP BEEP BEEP BEEP BEEP.* I looked at the screen on my forearm. Debris alarm.

Debris alarm? Already? Had I been out here that long? Or was the conjunction ahead of schedule?

Didn't matter why.

I tapped the screen to acknowledge and quiet the alarm, then jammed my controls forward. I had to hurry. Even though I was going all screwy, I was at least headed in the generally correct direction. I had to get over to the Quest air lock. And fast.

Uh-oh, no, I was losing control and going off course. If I couldn't hit the ISS, I'd have to abort and retract back to the *Aether* and leave the adults behind. There wasn't enough time or fuel for a second attempt.

The suits have a thin layer of material meant to protect from the tiniest of micrometeorites, but I knew that what was coming around for us was much too big for my suit to handle.

Something zipped past me like a glint of light, a shooting star gone in a millisecond. At the same time, a piece of the radiator array hanging down near Quest shattered and tiny shards spun in the sunlight, blasting toward me.

I'm too late. I have to abort.

I hesitated.

Dang it, I should just go for it.

Then the most terrifying thing of all happened. Probably even worse than a piece of debris just taking off my head. I jerked and snapped forward, flipping in a never-ending somersault but with a twisting motion that completely befuddled my sense of direction.

That was when I realized my tether had snapped.

Maybe a piece of debris had sliced through it and severed the cable.

As I spun, I saw the ISS, then Earth, then the *Aether*, then open space, then the ISS, then open space, then the *Aether*, then Earth . . .

I was adrift, spinning uncontrollably, and I knew I was moving away from both ships, toward Earth. My breathing was practically at hyperventilating level. I mashed on the thruster sticks to try to regain my attitude, but I only made it worse.

Then I noticed water leaking in my suit. I wriggled and shook my head, but it was clinging to my face, sloshing around over my eyes, my ears, my nose. I snorted, trying to keep a breathing hole. As ludicrous as it sounds, I thought, *Am I going to drown . . . in space?*

Another alarm went off. I blinked away the water for a second, long enough to see it was my oxygen warning sensor. My lungs were working hard, but it was more than just exertion or fear. It was like I was on top of Mount Everest. My head hurt.

I had a leak in my suit. I had been hit.

Spinning, water clouding my vision, my chest on fire, I knew I was going to die.

I knew I'd never see my parents again.

Chapter 28

Now you're all caught up on my story.

From here on out, neither of us knows what's going to happen. Freaky, right? But that's just life.

Hopefully, mine doesn't end in death-by-drowning-in-space. That'd probably be a first.

I knew I'd make the record books, but I never in a million years suspected it would be as the first person to drown in space. That's just silly.

I mean, I can still breathe enough for now. I'm not struggling as much anymore. Partly because I'm exhausted, but also because it won't do any good. I'm giving in and letting the tumble take me.

Yes, I'm still spinning and twisting, and the strobing visions of light and dark are making me kind of queasy. Throwing up in my suit would be—well, the way things are going, I have to say it wouldn't surprise me.

And I definitely don't want to join David in the

Vomitnaut Club.

I close my eyes and try to relax my body. I conserve my breaths. Even though it seems so obvious—that this is my end—I'm trying to trick myself into thinking that it's not.

Because I don't want it to end. It's that simple. This *can't* be the end of my story.

I know my life's not perfect. Far from it. Even though I maybe like to pretend to other people that it is. But I still want to live it.

I want to go home. I want to see my parents again, and Uncle D. I still have so many projects I want to finish. A lot has happened to our family in the last year. To me and, yes, to them. Because, of course, the bad stuff with Mom's plane accident happened to them too. As obvious as it seems to me now, I don't think I've acknowledged that it wasn't just about me, about what it did to me. It's what it did to *us*.

It can't be too late to tell them I'm sorry for pulling away.

My heart speeds up again. I know that will only burn through my faint oxygen faster, but I can't help it. All this pent-up anger and frustration boils around inside, and I erupt. With a scream.

"*Aaaaaaahhhhhhh!!*"

Oh, wow, that feels good. I do it again.

"*Aaaaaahhhhh!!*" It makes me even more light-headed, but with fists shaking and legs kicking, I scream until my throat is raw.

A good, long, hard scream that no one will ever hear. And with this water in the suit, no one will see my tears either.

Feels oddly freeing to be trapped out here in space where no one can hear me scream.

I inhale a sharp breath. My eyes snap open, and I have stars in my vision, even through the film of liquid stuck to my eyeballs. I don't mean the celestial stars. I mean the little squiggles that indicate you're about to pass out.

And then, out of the blue, I have a moment of odd lucidity. I remember what Uncle D said:

The hardest part is being honest with yourself.

I realize, with that scream, I'm being honest with myself right now. For maybe the first time, I'm being honest about how I feel about the accident.

I'm mad. And I'm sad. Such simple words, but I've only been trying to run away from them.

I mean, I haven't screamed like that in . . . ever? And so, even though I'm probably about to die, I do feel . . . sort of . . . *free*?

All it took was a little impending death to snap me out of it.

"It's okay," I say out loud, trying to manifest it. It sounds half-hearted because it is. The last words of a dying kid in space.

The rest of what Uncle D said comes to me now too:

And once you figure that out, the next-hardest part is telling someone you can trust.

So, I guess, that's why I wanted to tell this story. So someone knew it before I died. So my parents knew it.

Here I am, the real me, suspended above Earth, from which I ached to escape, now wishing I could spend just a few more minutes down on it with the people I love.

You know how sometimes when you're crying and then you start laughing and it's this weird mix of both? I'm laughing at myself, at my sentimental tears, that it took such a dramatic turn of events in my life to make me remember what's truly important. I choke on some water, which makes me laugh-cry some more.

And now I feel almost . . . What is that, *happy*? Some weird twisted version of *joy*? How in the heck could I be feeling joyful right now? Because I know what I want?

I shout again, but this time it's a happy whoop. Then I cough some more, wheezing with the lack of oxygen.

Then it passes, and I settle down. Floating. Staring at the Earth below. So sacredly beautiful.

Hey, do you know how astronauts say they're sorry? They apollo-gize.

We don't really say sorry much in my family. When you have a jet fighter pilot parent, you learn to hide when it hurts. I mean, every time she goes away, she might not be coming home. That's just too much potential hurt to acknowledge. So you lie to yourself about it, your teachers lie to you about it, and especially your parents lie to you about it. They say that of course everything will be fine and she'll be home safe any day now. They never talk about how an engine could catch fire and force an *Eject Eject* at Mach 1 that causes a terrible, spine-cracking paralysis.

Gentle, friendly little lies that you hear so often, you just expect them to come true every time.

None of this matters now. I shake my drowsy head. Sleep sounds so nice. I'm drifting, and drifting off. I feel warm.

It's okay. I feel okay now. Truly.

Enough! You had a cry. Now knock it off. Wouldn't it be SAFER to use your ejection seat? It's my mom's voice coming straight into my skull. She's not being mean. She's trying to save me.

"But I can't. I failed."

I blink my eyes like I'm just waking up and late for school. My head is so foggy. Maybe I'm sick and can stay home today.

I go to rub my eyes, and my hands thunk into my helmet. That's when I remember I'm floating. In space.

I remember David, Mae, and Kal back on the *Aether*. I remember five human beings trapped on the ISS that need me. I remember Uncle Dennis.

At the bottom of my vision, I catch a blurry flash of red. I look down through the fuzziness and see a blinking light on the control box of my SAFER thrusters.

Funny, I don't remember that being a part of the design—

Kal's software mod! The Automatic Attitude Hold! I flip the switch and immediately feel Kal's software take over, squirting whooshes of air this way and that, automatically adjusting my attitude, trying to counteract the wicked cartwheeling and twisting I'm doing. My legs and arms flail around like a possessed bull rider's, but eventually the horizon stops bobbing around and levels out, and the red light turns green.

I'm still. I'm stable.

"Ha!" I bark out loud. It worked.

My chest still burns from the low oxygen. If there's a tear in my suit, that's what is leaking pressure into space. My life-support backpack is trying to counteract the escaping atmosphere, but it's losing. It makes it very hard to focus.

In a reflection inside my visor, I see my mom. It's a hallucination and I shake it away, but I realize I don't have much time left before I lose my mind completely.

The water still clings to my face. I snort or spit when it gets in my nose or my mouth. The water in my ears makes it seem more like I'm underwater scuba diving than high up in orbit, but it's a very similar experience at this point given the water in my suit.

Except it's getting hotter too. The sun is up, and my liquid-cooled ventilation garment isn't doing its job.

That's it! The garment must be the source of the leak. So if the thing that is saving me from overheating isn't doing its job, then—

Oh, whatever, enough guessing which terrible thing will be my demise. I drown. I burn. I suffocate. What's the difference?

At least I'm not spinning anymore. I see the ISS ahead of me. I have to get over there.

Moving my arm to the SAFER control joystick is like pushing through honey. I'm weak and tired, and my body is shaking. I nudge the thruster. The acceleration, though slight, confuses my body. My inner ear starts spinning. I'm not actually in a roll again, but I'm suffering wicked vertigo all the same. I let go of the thruster.

I can't take a full breath, only shallow little slurps when what I want is a big gulp.

I'm fading.

"I got you!" The words are loud inside my head.

I know it's just another hallucination, but I respond

anyway because it's my mom. "Mom?"

My body jolts, like the ejection seat in my dream. Well, a bit softer than that but nearly as sudden and surprising. It's the SAFER firing into my back even though I didn't trigger it.

I reach for the controls. The system must be going haywire, but I can't wrap my fist around the joystick.

I try to speak, to ask my mom what she's doing, what is going on, but my words are gibberish.

"Can't let you get away without a rematch of asteroid-moon-planet." A different voice. Definitely not my mom. A male voice. *Dad?*

"Out there hogging all the spotlight," he says. No, not Dad. I wake up a little when I realize who it is: *David.*

"We've got you, Fin." It's Mae's voice this time. The voice I thought was my mom.

"Hey, Fin." Now Kal is on the mic. "Did you hear about the claustrophobic astronaut?"

Yes. I know this one. But my lips are thick and my throat is scratchy and I can barely think.

"He just needed a little space!"

I remember telling her that joke way back during training.

I must be hallucinating again, because the comms aren't working, so I shouldn't be hearing their voices in my head. But someone or something is clearly controlling my suit. Unless that is a hallucination too. I'm really lost if that's true, because the delta-vee sure feels real.

The screen on my forearm is too fuzzy; I can't make out what it's telling me. I can't think clearly.

The SAFER is still firing, moving me closer to a silver blur that I know is the ISS.

"We're going to fly you to the Quest air lock, Fin." Kal, or whoever is driving this thing, guides me through what is happening. "When you get there, all you need to do is hang on tight to the hull and wait for rescue. Commander Horowitz and Pilot Gurkin will haul you in. Okay?"

Okay, this must be happening for real. That is way too specific for a hallucination. I don't have any idea how, but I'm rolling with it. I have to.

I respond, but it's more of a grunt. I think they get the gist.

"Another surprise from Kal, Fin. She installed remote-control software for the SAFER when she uploaded the AAH." It's David. His words are like a gift I never had on my wish list. "She didn't want to say anything, because she's not actually done with it, but I'm currently playing you with a video game controller."

A video game controller. Ha! I must have laughed out loud because I hear a cheer and a "woo-hoo!" in response from my friends.

I'm flying through space, grateful for Kal's little surprises. Her code has saved my life twice now in a matter of minutes. The most pivotal few minutes of my life, no doubt.

It's like I'm being hoisted on their shoulders, and the thrill of it pumps new adrenaline through my veins, a tiny bit of last strength pushing me to stay awake.

Don't pass out yet.

With David, the gamer, guiding me in, I just have to hold on. We can do this.

The blur gets closer. I raise my arms, ready to grab onto anything I can.

My chest feels like it is being constricted by a boa, requiring a ton of effort to inhale every tiny breath. Not to mention the salty water of my sweat stinging my eyes and distracting my focus.

The SAFER's thrusters sputter and die. Out of fuel. I knew we had one shot at this. I'm coasting in the right direction, at an angle to the ISS, getting closer.

Closer. Almost there . . .

I can do this.

"Now, Fin! Grab on!" Mae, shouting in my ear.

And *BAM*, I slam into the ISS.

"Oof!" It jars my bones. I bounce, ricocheting from the collision.

Arms flailing, I scrabble away from the Quest node

wall, gloved hands reaching to get a grip of anything on the blurry gray surface before I float too far away and lose my last shot.

Grabbing, grabbing, grabbing, sliding down the metal toward the empty void.

My feet hit a railing at the end of the node, and I hope for a split second, but then they slip.

Then my right hand catches something, a loose wire, and I close my fist with all my might and loop it around my palm so it won't slip out, and then my body jolts. Hard. My shoulder aches, but I'm still holding on to a cable at the very end of the module. It springs me back, my momentum reversed, and I yo-yo toward the hull.

I can't rest yet. My heart is still racing, every breath a battle. I have to take advantage of the adrenaline before it wears off, so I climb. I hoist myself along the cable until I reach the metal surface of the ISS.

More with feel than sight, I pull myself along to what I know is the handrailing circling the air lock. I pat the hatch until I find the handle. I twist with all my might. But it's stuck. Or I'm too weak. Or both.

I think back to undocking the *Aether* after it had suffered damage to the docking mechanism. I needed David's help there. But I'm not getting that help this time.

I put two hands on it and try again, screaming into

my helmet. I won't stop fighting.

To my surprise, the hatch pops inward and I am flung into the ISS, knocking my helmet hard enough against the side of the opening that it cracks the glass. Water squirts out of my helmet into the air lock.

I'm not all the way in. There's a tug at my back and the vibrations of something scraping along the hatch opening.

The other space suit! I forgot all about that thing. It's still attached to me.

The extra suit is slowing me down from entering fully, and I'm out of time. I know I can't jettison the suit or someone on the ISS will die.

I'm completely drained and have no idea how I manage it, but I do: I pull myself and the rest of the extra suit into the air lock. I close the hatch, sealing myself into the damaged ISS, and then I completely stop moving. I smile lethargically because I'm still alive. I made it!

Then—I stop breathing.

I can't make out who it is, but I see a shadowy movement through the tiny porthole into the ISS. It's dark in there. The squiggly pinwheels in my vision increase, meaning I'm going to pass out any second.

Kal comes on the radio. "You did it, Fin! Commander Horowitz and Pilot Gurkin are doing an emergency pressurization of the crew lock. Just hang on a little longer. Please."

So close. I've come this close, but I'm not going to make it. I can't wait. I'm not breathing. And I can't tell anyone.

My body shakes. The endorphins are wearing off, and I can't do anything but spasm.

An alert tone chimes. I see a faint green light through the haze of my vision and my throbbing head, then I feel a pressure differential push on my suit, implying the other hatch has opened. Then hands all over me, pulling me into the ISS. Then my helmet twisting off.

Hands on my neck. Then someone compressing my chest, pushing repeatedly. I hear my name, and suddenly my body reacts.

I inhale with greedy gusto like it's my first breath as a baby.

I hold it for a second, then exhale through my mouth and breathe again, this time through my nose. I smell burnt steak. I remember an astronaut describe how the vacuum in the air lock pulls trace elements out of the metal of the ship. That metallic "smell of space" people talk about is actually more just the smell of the ship than actual space.

And I laugh because why in the heck am I thinking about *that* right now? And I laugh because who cares? I'm alive!

I take another huge, conscious breath. Though the

ISS air is stale, it's the sweetest breath I've ever had.

And I cry too, this time from the pure joy and exhilaration of that breath.

I am alive.

I am cold, shivering.

Someone rubs a towel over my face, through my hair.

Someone hugs me. And I pass out.

Chapter 29

"That SAFER unit is quite the invention, Fin," Pilot Gurkin says to me. It's the first full sentence I hear when I wake up. It feels misplaced. I'm expecting something calmer, less enthusiastic, since my head is pounding.

It makes me want to go back to sleep, but our bubbly pilot won't let me.

"You had us worried out there!" she says.

"It was Kal's software that saved me." I rub my eyes. I'm not shaking. I'm warm, out of my suit and wrapped in a silver Mylar blanket.

The other three *Aether* crew—Commander Horowitz, Specialists Barrera and Sokolov—greet me, and for a second I think I'm back on the *Aether*.

Then I remember, and it steals my breath.

I'm on the doomed ISS, oxygen running low, with who knows how long until—

"The debris." I sit up and cough, panicked. "We have

to get out of here."

Pilot Gurkin gives me a warm smile, like she knows something I don't.

It's mostly dark on the ISS. Emergency lights dot the walls, but the station is obviously on backup power supply. I have no idea how long that will last.

Why is she smiling?

"That was a foolish thing you did, Fin." Commander Horowitz has his arms crossed. "You not only put yourself in extreme danger, but you've put the rest of the kids' lives at risk as well. You know that."

"Were we just supposed to leave you out here to die?" I can feel my face going hot.

"If that's what happens, so be it," the commander says, very matter-of-factly.

Pilot Gurkin nods and puts her hand on my shoulder. "We know the risks."

"But we can save you." At least, I thought we could before my suit got shredded. "Did the other EMU get damaged too? The extra I brought over?"

"It has some minor scuffs, but it's still flight-ready." Specialist Barrera pats the suit hanging next to four others.

A total of five suits.

But there are five people left on the ISS, plus me. That's six total.

We're still one suit short.

Because my suit got ruined during the crossing, I hadn't changed anything. Well, I'd added my own name to the list of the doomed.

I look around at the people staring at me, thinking that one of these people is going to draw the short straw and be left behind.

Wait. I count the faces watching me.

"There are only four of you," I say. "There should be five. Did you cram someone extra on one of the Soyuz? Why only one?"

The crew members eye one another. They look tired.

"What?" I ask. "Why are there only four of you when there should be five left behind?"

Commander Horowitz delivers the news. "We sent your four guardians, Commander Smith, and Engineer Morales down on the Soyuz capsules. But that left only the four of us here, the *Aether* crew, because Science Officer Christa Allaire . . . She didn't make it. Unfortunately, I'm sorry to say, Christa sustained fatal injuries when the fire blew out the Harmony module."

What? She's . . . dead?

"No. That can't be true. I'm here to save her."

Christa. Our fun-loving tour guide.

Uncle D and the other guardians made it, though. I should be relieved. They're probably safely back on Earth by now.

Still, we lost Christa. I hate it.

I look around at the remaining crew, pity in their eyes like I'm some little kid they have to protect. "No more. We're not losing anyone else."

"Of course not." Pilot Gurkin squeezes where her hand is on my shoulder. I know she wants to be sincere and comforting, but it feels like another one of those little lies adults tell so easily. She doesn't know that it's going to be okay. None of us does.

I don't want to be rude, but I move myself away from her. "You don't know that. You can't know. There are still five of us here. Debris. Low oxygen. Trapped in a broken space station with only five suits—"

And then a grim thought occurs to me, accompanied by an immediate pang of guilt for thinking it.

Five suits. With Christa gone, there are only five of us here on the ISS. Christa losing her life may have actually saved one of ours.

We could actually still escape the ISS together.

"She died so that we can live," I say. I look Commander Horowitz in the eye. "There are now five of us. And five operational suits."

"Your friends told us about your plan, Fin," Pilot Gurkin says. "But since your tether was severed during the crossing, there's no zip-lining for us today." She smiles. Why would she smile while saying that?

"You're lucky that hole in your suit wasn't bigger, or you wouldn't have made it this far," Specialist Barrera says. "You'd be toast."

Commander Horowitz shoots him the stink eye. "Glenn."

"What?" Barrera says. "It's the truth."

"You fixed the oxygen problem? What about the debris?" I ask.

"Well, we have the suits for breathing. That will last us long enough to witness the reentry, but that assumes the debris doesn't get us first," Barrera answers.

Commander Horowitz pulls himself closer to me. "I admire your bravery, Fin. I really do. But you should have listened to Houston. You should have raised your orbit to get out of the debris field. I've ordered the *Aether* to do just that."

Oh no.

I look back, hoping to see the *Aether* out of a window, but there's no window to look out of. I imagine my ship and my friends on the other side of this thin wall, thrusting to safety. My lifeboat is leaving me. My skin chills.

"But they're not listening to me either," the commander says. His lips are tight, but I can tell he is finally cracking, letting a little emotion through, a mix between frustration and sorrow. And the way he puffs his chest, with pride.

One giant leap. Mae's words come to me. One giant leap. "Was the SAFER damaged?"

"Surprisingly, no. At least, not that I could see from visual inspection," Dr. Sokolov replies.

"Can you refill it?" I ask, perking up.

"Well, yes, but what do you think you're going to do with it?" Dr. Sokolov looks to Horowitz, who narrows his eyes at me.

"Everyone suit up. We're getting out of here." My turn to smile.

"What are you talking about?" Specialist Barrera asks.

"That other suit is big for you, Fin," Dr. Sokolov says. "We could adjust it down, but it'll still be bulky on you since it's a full adult size. Your custom EMU, the one that was irreparably damaged, was only built so you could have the honor of testing the SAFER."

"That's okay, since the SAFER can still attach to any of our backpacks," I say. "Right?" I am already stepping into my new suit.

Specialist Barrera lights up. "He's right."

"But there's only one SAFER. And you, Fin, are going to take it and fly back to the *Aether* and get out of here." Commander Horowitz points away. "That's an order."

"No way," I reply. "I'm taking everyone with me. I'll tow you across to the *Aether*." I continue suiting up, not waiting for him to tell me it's a foolish idea. "I'll tow you. It'll work."

Then, under my breath, I add, "It has to."

"It might," Specialist Barrera says. "But maybe you should be our pilot, Eileen."

Commander Horowitz is silent. I can see he's gritting his teeth by the way the muscles in his jaw tense. Finally, he speaks. "No, the kid should get the SAFER life jacket. In case something goes sideways, we'll unclip and let him get to safety."

And so, it is decided. We're doing this together.

Specialist Barrera pumps his fist. Pilot Gurkin hugs Dr. Sokolov. They rush to their suits and start gearing up for the craziest, riskiest, most awesome adventure they might ever have in their lives. And these are astronauts, so that's saying a lot.

Or we'll get lost in the vacuum of space and die alone, drifting forever and ever through the vast endlessness of the universe.

But hopefully not that.

Chapter 30

We have to depressurize the equipment lock portion of Quest too, since there are five of us and we won't all fit in the tiny crew lock that leads to outside. As Horowitz shuts the hatch to the rest of the ISS, I notice he pauses for a second and looks back inside with a sigh. I guess he's saying goodbye. And it occurs to me that we will be the last humans to ever visit the International Space Station.

I feel like I should salute or something.

While the crew suited up, I ate a snack and drank a protein drink. Despite almost dying, I'm not physically hurt at all. After some oxygen and some food, I feel mostly recovered. And now, with the SAFER unit on my back and a tether attached to the other four astronauts like a train, I feel more in control than ever. Plus, with that little scream I had (that we will never speak of again), I feel almost—hopeful?

I mean, I've been out there and done this once

already. I can do it again.

Sure, I flubbed it last time and had to be saved by David on the video game controller using Kal's software, but hey, second time's the charm, right? I feel confident that I can do better this time. And knowing I have someone on backup remote doesn't hurt either.

Commander Horowitz is stretched out beside me in the crew lock, staring through his visor directly at me. It's kinda creepy.

"What?" I finally ask.

"Your parents must be very proud. You're a remarkable young man."

I smirk and scoff. My parents tell me they're proud of me often, sure. But sometimes I don't feel like I deserve it, like it's another one of those little lies. The old me, the kid who existed before almost dying in space, probably would have replied with something snarky like "Of course." But I don't feel like being that kid right now. Or maybe ever again.

And I'm not really sure how to be this new me yet either.

"Thanks" is all I can say. And I mean it too.

He gives a little nod and checks his watch.

"Commander Horowitz," I say, "I've always been curious about something. Maybe you can answer for me?"

"Sure." He gives another nod.

"Why aren't astronauts hungry when they get to space?"

"Uh," he says. "I'm not sure I've heard of that experience."

Dr. Sokolov snickers.

"Because they just had a big launch," I tell him.

Horowitz looks at me blankly for a second, but when Dr. Sokolov busts out a laugh, he finally realizes it's a joke.

I'm very proud to say that not only did I get him to smile, but I made the stoic *Aether* commander *laugh*.

An alert tone chimes and the Quest air lock light turns red, indicating that depressurization has completed. Horowitz opens the hatch, and sunlight streams into the near darkness of our air lock. Horowitz flips down his sun visor, and I follow his lead.

Which reminds me: "Hey, why didn't the sun go to college?"

"I know this one too!" Dr. Sokolov blurts over the comms.

"I don't know. Why?" Horowitz plays along, prepared for a joke this time.

"Because it already has 27 million degrees!"

Man, that one is a groaner. I mean, I literally hear Barrera groan.

"After you, pilot." Horowitz gestures to the outside.

The *Aether* floats in the near distance. It's probably only a hundred feet away, but at the same time it seems so much farther.

"I'm scared," I say, so suddenly that I surprise myself. I can't remember the last time I ever actually said *that* out loud.

Casually, without missing a beat, Commander Horowitz replies, "That's good." He pats me on the back. "You have some precious cargo here."

I breathe in, breathe out, and hold my hand in front of my face. I remember sitting on the launchpad and watching it shake. But here, now, about to do this insane thing with all these lives at stake, my hand isn't shaking. Doesn't mean I'm not scared, but my hand isn't shaking. I'm not sure what to make of that.

I hear a polite cough from the commander. Right, to business.

I reach out and clip my tether to the railing on the external wall of the station, then shove myself out toward Earth.

The plan is that we'll get outside the air lock first, then push off in sequence. And of course, I'll tow us over with bursts from the SAFER. If things go haywire, David and Kal are on standby to help remotely. Mae is controlling the *Aether*'s position, ready to intercept if we get too far off course.

This must be how a quarterback feels, the whole

team following his lead.

As the astronauts shimmy their way out, I watch Earth flow by below: the swirling patterns of the clouds, what looks like a wide river of smoke from a wildfire or volcano extending far into the sea, the thin blue line of our atmosphere holding in all the precious air we need to thrive. It is so cool to see. I can't imagine this view ever getting old. And, despite everything that's happened, I am reminded how lucky I am to get to see it.

Everyone is out. The five of us are tethered together, crouched on the nadir side of the ISS, ready to pounce into open space and away from the dying station.

"Standing by," David and Kal say in unison, confirming they are ready to take over via remote control, if need be.

"Ready," Mae says, confirming she is prepared to fly the *Aether* as close as possible to grab us.

The ISS air lock door is still open, but there's no going back. Ever.

"Okay, to get some momentum, we'll all want to push off as strong as we can, in sequence," Horowitz says. "Fin first. For the rest of us, we don't want to get ahead of Fin. So, Fin, I'll let your tether play out a bit, then I'll lock my cable connected to you and jump. You'll be pulling me at that point, so you'll feel a tug when I do that. Okay?"

"Roger that," I say.

"Then Sokolov, then Gurkin, then our caboose," the commander finishes.

"Caboose is an important job," Specialist Barrera replies.

"And might be your new call sign," Pilot Gurkin teases.

"If we survive this, you can call me whatever you want," he says.

I unclip but keep my handhold tight. I am ready. I have to do this. I exhale from my mouth.

Now. I have to go now.

Quick, don't think.

Just leap.

One giant leap.

"Okay, here I go in three . . . two . . . one!"

The muscles in my quads spring, and I am flying.

Hands on the SAFER controls, I give a quick shot of propellant to course correct. It's already awkward to steer the joysticks in bulky gloves, but these adult-size ones just make it even harder to control, to even feel the joystick in my hand.

"Here I come." It's Horowitz over the comms, cool and calm.

Horowitz jumps. Okay, good, we're doing this.

"Locking my cable," Horowitz warns.

Oof! That's more than a little tug from behind. I

wobble. I push on the thrusters to keep the forward movement.

This feeling repeats itself as Sokolov, then Gurkin, then Barrera join the train, but the feeling is multiplied as each of our forces bounces us around with equal and opposite reactions. I'm fighting hard to maintain control. I really want to do this on my own, without David's help this time.

We're moving closer to the *Aether*, but it feels like only inches are going by as I tug these wobbly weights behind me.

I blink, and a flash of Christa's face surprises me.

How did she die? I wonder. Doesn't matter right now. I close my eyes to take a breath, and I see a bright flash.

I recoil and let go of the thrusters. Was that another cosmic ray? Was it Christa?

It makes me think of what we've lost. It makes me think of what I almost lost back home.

Time crawls. We're using way more propellant than I thought we'd need.

I'm off course. Not by a lot, but Mae tells us she's going to scoot down to meet our current trajectory. I acknowledge. There's still shrapnel from the busted solar arrays and scaffolding wobbling around, so she has to be very careful not to get too close.

Psh psh pshhhhh. I see the spray from the *Aether* thrusters.

It's a feat of master maneuvering when she gets clear of those pieces from the ISS.

"Almost there," the commander says. "Steady as she goes, Fin. You're doing great."

I am doing great. But I can't celebrate yet.

Almost there.

All that's left is the last ten yards when Kal comes over the comms with urgency in her voice. "The ISS truss cracked! It's swinging toward the *Aether*! Evasive action!"

I can't see behind me, but if I'm going to be impaled by space junk, there's not much I can do about it now. I wonder if the field of space debris has come around again, if it's peppering the ISS and that's what caused a new break.

My throat suddenly feels tight again, and I gasp for air. There's no water in my suit, but I'm flashing back to how I almost drowned in space.

I recognize it's just my imagination and jam the thruster control forward. No way is this how this story ends, so close to success.

Mae is firing and rolling the *Aether*, and I see the truss assembly come into the top of my field of view. It's a long chunk of twisted metal, spinning end over end, cartwheeling right over us and straight for the *Aether*.

It's definitely going to hit. I can't do anything but

watch as it careens toward my friends.

Mae is a great pilot, though, and she flies the *Aether* so precisely that the metal bars of scaffolding spin right around the *Aether*, missing by what looks to be centimeters. I exhale so heavily that I fog up my visor. It quickly clears, and I realize that because of the *Aether*'s moves, we're off course again.

It happened so fast, and now our momentum is going to carry us above the *Aether*.

The SAFER jets sputter. The propellant is almost out, and I'm running on fumes.

The *Aether* air lock is approaching fast, but we're still too high. I try to reverse the thruster to slow us down, but the SAFER quits. That's it.

We're adrift. And too high.

We're going to sail right past the *Aether*. My heart pounds like a jackhammer.

Maybe Mae can follow us. Maybe she can catch up with us. I hold on to that hope.

I push on the SAFER controls, praying for a bit more juice, but nothing.

I zing right past the *Aether* and now all I see are the bright white stars speckled in the dark black onyx of space.

I've failed. Again.

At least this will be the last time.

Chapter 31

Oof! I'm snapped nearly in half by a sudden jerk. I reach down and use the cable to spin myself around. I see Horowitz down the line from me, then Sokolov and Gurkin, and the most welcome sight I think I'll ever see. Holding on to the railing of the *Aether* air lock by one hand is Specialist Barrera.

"Nice work, caboose!" Pilot Gurkin cheers over the radio.

"Told you. The caboose is an important job," Barrera replies. There's strain in his voice. He grunts. "Better reel yourselves down here. I could use some help. I think that tug dislocated my shoulder."

I notice his right arm is dangling. His left hand is the only thing holding our human train to the railing. He can't clip in without letting go, since his right arm is now useless.

I push the button on my tether to start reeling myself toward Horowitz like a caught fish. The others are all doing the same, so we're approaching the *Aether* together. Gurkin connects with the hull first and clips us in.

We are now attached to the *Aether*. We're no longer sailing in open space.

We did it.

I can't believe it for a second.

Unless something else goes wrong, we did it. We escaped the wreck of the ISS.

After some jostling, we're inside the *Aether* air lock. It's a tight fit for five of us, but we're here. Horowitz spins the air lock hatch closed and kicks off the pressurization. It's pushing on our suits and feels glorious. Like victory. A pressurized embrace of safety.

Back in the *Aether* cabin and out of our suits, David slugs my shoulder in a friendly way. Kal hugs me and tucks the strand of purple hair behind her ear with a grin. Mae even gives me a nod. I can tell they respect what I've done, but it goes both ways. Each of them played an important role in saving the *Aether* crew from the ISS. In saving me.

We couldn't have done it without one another.

Once the initial celebration has tapered off, I watch the ISS from the big windows at the nose of the *Aether*. The station is hardly recognizable as that bug I saw floating in space when we arrived not so long ago. The whoosh of a fireball erupts from what I guess is an oxygen tank or something. The fire in space is actually kind of cool, a sphere that flutters and oscillates, the flame disappearing and reappearing until it's burned itself out.

Pilot Gurkin takes over from Mae. As she moves the *Aether* away from the ISS, the marvel of engineering continues to tear into bits. Wreckage begets wreckage. More of the modules are torn open, and the resulting debris smashes into itself, making even more debris. Some of this will float off as space junk, but I hope the bulk of it is headed for incineration in Earth's atmosphere.

After almost three decades of service to the world, the once-mighty ISS will burn.

Science Officer Christa Allaire, still on board, will go down with her ship.

"Burned up like a Viking pyre," David says proudly, then adds something in his native Norwegian. "Frykt ikke døden, for den tiden din undergang er satt, og ingen kan unnslippe den."

Mae cozies up to David, and he puts his arm around her. "What does it mean?" she asks.

"It's from the Völsunga saga. 'Fear not death, for the hour of your doom is set and none may escape it.'"

Chapter 32

So, what now?

We're inside the *Aether*. Safe, it seems. We've escaped the doomed ISS *and* saved the astronauts; it seems like we're out of danger. We should go home, hug our parents, bask in the inevitable media attention for our next fifteen minutes of fame, and then that's it. Right?

I had my scream in space and got that out of my system. Finally. I learned a lesson, I survived, end of story.

Then why don't I feel like this is truly the end?

I know a lot has happened to me, to us, and yet there's still something nagging at me.

I peek around at my shipmates. Can they see through me? Do they know I cried out there?

They're not looking at me. David and Mae are still watching the ISS, its fiery death plunge lighting up the atmosphere, his arm around her, her head leaning on his shoulder.

Kal, Pilot Gurkin, and Dr. Sokolov stare at one of the screens. Kal points at something, and Dr. Sokolov nods. Pilot Gurkin has her smile back and is looking at Kal with a gleam of pride like I bet Kal wishes her dad would.

Commander Horowitz is on the comms with Houston and scratching his chin in thought. Specialist Barrera is sitting beside the commander, with headphones on, listening, staring at Horowitz as if he doesn't like what he's hearing.

The eight of us survived. So why don't I feel . . . what? Alive? Maybe I didn't make it out there. Maybe I'm a ghost. But would a ghost feel hungry?

I grab a protein bar and open the crinkly wrapper.

Kal hears me and eyes my food. "I would kill for some dosas right now. With mango chutney." She rubs her belly.

I offer her a protein bar. "Isn't that like a crepe?"

"Kinda, but better." She grins and takes the offered lump of sustenance shaped into a bar.

"I could go for some meatballs," David says. "But I'll just pretend while I chew on this tar." He opens a snack too.

Horowitz pulls off his headphones and gathers us around for a debriefing. After puffing us up by acknowledging Mae's excellent flying skills and our "heroic bravery in the face of extreme odds," he tells us the bad news.

"The diagnostic checks report that some of the thruster quads are damaged," he says.

"We knew that," Mae says.

"The remaining thrusters can maintain our attitude, though. The damage isn't enough to negatively affect overall flight operations," Pilot Gurkin quickly adds, noting that redundancy is built in to the systems so as to minimize the effects of one, or even a few, defective units. "However, the fact that they are damaged indicates that other areas of the ship may have been hit too." She clasps her hands together and pauses, letting that sink in.

Dr. Sokolov pipes up, apparently trying to counterbalance the warning. "Life-support systems show nominal. Propellant levels are lower than where we planned to be at this time in the mission, from Mae's excellent evasive maneuvers, but we still have more than enough battery power to survive up here for a while."

When she says that—"survive up here for a while"— we kids look at one another.

"A while?" Kal asks, pausing midchew.

"The good news," Commander Horowitz continues, "is that all six of the astronauts who escaped in the Soyuz capsules have been picked out of the ocean by the Navy's USS *Dragon* and are safe on board. Your guardians are safe." He smiles, and I can tell it's a relief for him too. He was responsible for them, after all.

"With steaming mugs of hot chocolate," Pilot Gurkin adds, pretending to sniff an imaginary cup of hot cocoa between two hands.

I breathe a sigh for Uncle D and peer out the window at Earth. We're flying over ocean again, and I can't help but give a little wave down to him.

Kal chuckles at my gesture, but she joins in. It somehow brings them closer, I guess.

I think of my parents too. They must know I'm okay. They must have been worried sick.

I know what it's like to think you're going to lose a loved one, or to think you've already lost them, like when we got the news of Mom's accident at the airfield. Then later, hearing she was still alive, I was so immensely relieved to know she was okay, but it never really fully cleared the lingering fear that she almost wasn't going to be around anymore. How life can change in an instant.

Looking down at Earth, I think I *should* feel like going back home. But I don't, really, not yet. I mean, I want to go home eventually, but right now, I still have this pestering urge, floating here, like I have unfinished business and it's not time yet.

After everything that has happened, I'm not ready to return and just go back to my life as it was. I . . . can't.

This journey isn't over.

"Houston asked us to prepare for an EVA," Horowitz says.

"To look for damage," Mae adds, "before a reentry attempt."

"Affirmative." Commander Horowitz points to Mae, all business. "We have to examine the *Aether*'s heat tiles for damage before attempting a reentry." The allusion to the *Columbia* disaster is obvious. "On the ISS, they were able to do an external visual inspection of the Soyuz capsules using the Canadarm2 robotic arm, but the *Aether* doesn't have anything like that. And we can't use the Canadarm2 anymore. So we'll have to do a manual inspection. If all tests pass, then we'll be returning home shortly."

The implication is clear what will happen if the tests don't pass . . . We'll have to "survive up here for a while."

"I'm sorry I can't do the walk," Barrera says, nodding to the sling on the shoulder he dislocated saving us. Fortunately, Dr. Sokolov says he'll be fine in a day or two. But no way could he do a space walk in his condition.

"I'll go," Commander Horowitz says.

"And me," Dr. Sokolov adds. "I'll do it."

Commander Horowitz and Dr. Sokolov put their EMUs back on and head out to inspect the *Aether*, while we watch the video feeds from their helmets.

As the commander pans around to view the side of our ship that will bear the intense 3,000 degrees of reentry, we see a bunch of black scorch marks pocking the hull. It doesn't look great, but it could simply be surface damage. Though something tells me that is wishful thinking.

Commander Horowitz works carefully with an oversize drill to remove a panel. It doesn't come up easily, and he has to pry it with both hands. He jerks and it loosens, sending him off-balance.

He goes flinging into space. I suck air through my teeth.

The tether holding him to the *Aether* unwinds and then slows his movement. He dangles at the end of it like a run-out yo-yo.

"I'm okay," he says calmly.

"I'm sure you've had enough of hanging from tethers in space!" Barrera jokes over the comms as the commander reels himself back in.

Dr. Sokolov grabs him when he's close, and they pause for a moment, helmet to helmet. We can see their faces up close. She nods. He nods back, confirming whatever unspoken thing was communicated between them.

Then they get back to work.

"The hexagonal heat shield tiles are obviously

damaged," the commander reports. "Multiple pieces of
the aluminum-lithium and carbon fiber slabs have
cracked or been raked by something. Probably
shrapnel from the ISS or space debris."

Our commander and doctor come back into the
Aether, depressurize, desuit, and explain what will
happen next.

"There's a repair kit on the *Aether* for this
eventuality, but given the extent of the damage, and
the clunkiness of working in space in a suit, I predict it
will take several space walks," the commander says.

"And maybe three days to fix the damaged tiles
before it's safe for us to reenter," Dr. Sokolov adds,
answering the obvious question we all have.

"Three days?" I'm not worried about life support,
but waiting here for three days sounds sort of . . .
boring. I snort air through my nose. Here I am, after
everything we've been through, describing my time in
space as *boring*. It has most definitely been anything
but that.

But still, I want to keep moving, like how some
sharks need to swim to keep the oxygen in the water
flowing over their gills, or they'll suffocate.

"Why don't we continue the mission?" Mae asks. I
point at her, then tap my nose.

Pilot Gurkin chuckles and smiles like Mae is making
a joke.

"Why not?" I ask, serious. "We're stable. Dr. Sokolov said that life support is nominal. Let's go to Gateway. And the Moon. Like we originally planned."

"Yeah, let's go," David adds. He puts up a fist for me to bump.

Commander Horowitz chuckles and shakes his head. "After everything that just happened? No way."

"Maybe *because* of everything that just happened, we *need* to go," I say. "We still have a mission, to drop off Specialists Sokolov and Barrera on the Gateway. We can't give up. Space is dangerous, but we can't quit because of what happened. What if NASA quit after the Apollo 1 disaster?"

Given that the Apollo 1 astronauts all died tragically, maybe that wasn't the best example.

"We can't give up," I add, trying to make my point.

That's true, but I'm also just not ready to return to Earth. That sounds harder than going to the Moon. Just thinking about what I might say to my parents, what I need to say, makes my chest tight. I'm not ready.

Night is coming around again on Earth, and the aurora sparkles in a brilliant, glimmering shimmer. I've never seen the northern lights from the surface, but up here they are unbelievable. The pictures don't capture the three-dimensionality. You have to see for yourself.

A pain shoots through my head, making me wince, and I put my hand to my temple.

"You all right?" Kal asks.

"Yeah, fine," I say. "Just a headache." I shake it off and drink some water.

"Commander," Mae says, "instead of orbiting Earth while you repair the heat shield, we may as well spend that time traveling toward the Moon, right? Three days to repair, three days to get to the Moon."

"My dad would not approve," Kal says.

Oh, great, dissension in the ranks.

Then she adds, grinning, "But I do. And the math works out." She points to her screen. "By my calculations, we have enough propellant to continue our mission within the margins of safety. I—I didn't think I'd say this, but—I want to go to the Moon."

"I'm down to go." David shrugs. "But what if there's more space junk out there?"

"Actually," Mae answers, "the farther we get from Earth, the less likely it is to encounter human-made junk. But, of course, the chance of micrometeoroids increases. And then there's the Van Allen belts of radiation."

"Not helping, Mae."

"Right." She stops.

Pilot Gurkin whispers something to Commander Horowitz, who then looks to Specialist Barrera and Dr. Sokolov. They both nod. The commander sighs, but with a smirk and a tilt of his head.

There's no way he's going to agree to this, I think, but he surprises us. "Okay. I'll ask Houston."

"Yes!" Mae pumps her fist.

Commander Horowitz gets on the comms and hails mission control. "Houston, the *Aether* has a request."

"Go, *Aether*."

"The *Aether* crew requests permission to proceed with our taxi service to drop off Mission Specialists Sokolov and Barrera on the Gateway outpost. Confirm approval?"

"Come again, *Aether*?"

"That's right, Houston," Commander Horowitz repeats. "The *Aether* and her crew would like to continue our mission to the Moon."

Silence for a few heartbeats.

"Uh, let us get back to you on that one, *Aether*." Houston clicks the comms off.

We all look at one another and then bust out laughing. Even ol' Horowitz laughs with us.

Chapter 33

About an hour later, the flight director herself comes on the line from Houston and asks us in a thick Texas accent, "Are y'all sure you want to do this? Commander, after the tragedy that occurred with the ISS, is your crew psychologically ready to go even farther into space and farther away from your home planet?"

The commander looks to us. "I think they've earned the right to answer that for themselves, Flight Director."

She forces us to go around and each declare individually that we have no reservations about continuing the mission.

"Roger that, Houston," Mae says first.

So Kal, David, and I take turns repeating after her: "Roger that, Houston."

"Well, then, *Aether*," the flight director says, "your parents have said that of course they'd much rather have you home, but since you can't return until the repairs are done anyway, and since the ship is in otherwise nominal condition, and because NASA supports getting Mission Specialists Barrera and Sokolov to Gateway, you hereby have the full blessing of mission control to conduct your trans-lunar injection burn and head to the Moon."

We cheer.

Mae hugs David.

I go to hug Kal, but she looks at me funny, and we do an awkward double-arm-pat thing.

We hear applause over the comms from the support personnel in Houston mission control.

With all the cheering, my headache is screaming. During the hour we were waiting, I sneaked some ibuprofen from the first aid kit and drank more water, but something doesn't feel right. My joints ache, and my head feels fuzzy.

I wonder if it's residual leftovers from nearly dying earlier. But there's no way I can ruin this celebration by saying anything. I don't want to be a downer.

Besides, how could I not be excited? I'm going to the Moon!

We buckle up for the trans-lunar injection burn, and I close my eyes, determined to not let my deteriorating physical condition dampen this decision.

Nothing I can do about it but wait it out anyway,

right? It's probably nothing serious.

Several hours after we cut off the burn and we're drifting through space, my head pounds harder and my elbows and knees feel bloated, painfully tender. I don't know what anyone can do, so I keep it to myself and do my best to soldier through. It'll pass.

While Commander Horowitz and Specialist Sokolov are out patching up our ship, Pilot Gurkin tests us on the Gateway outpost as a way to pass the time. We learned about the new station back in training at JSC, so we fare pretty well on her pop quiz.

"Kalpana, tell me about the Gateway's orbit?" she asks.

"Why me?" Kal says.

"I can tell you," I say. Despite my aches and pains, I can't pass up an opportunity to best a teammate.

"No, no," Kal says. "I know it."

I figured the competition would spur her on.

"The Gateway outpost," she answers, "orbits the Moon in a seven-day near-rectilinear halo orbit, an NRHO. That means it flies within 3,000 kilometers of the northern lunar pole, then out to 70,000 kilometers from the southern pole, in a big elliptical loop that takes about seven days for one round trip."

"Coincidence," David adds, "that it is one week, and Gateway is closest to the lunar surface on Mondays, which has origins as 'the day of the Moon' in Anglo-Saxon."

We all stare at him.

"What? I thought it was interesting."

I think it's interesting too, but it reminds me: "Want to hear a moon joke?"

David glares at me. "I think you're going to tell us anyway."

"Why is it so hard to be a werewolf on Jupiter?" I ask.

Pilot Gurkin looks like she's thinking.

"It has eighty moons!" Specialist Barrera answers.

"Yes, you're the winner! Ba-doom-pow." As soon as I make the drum motion, my shoulders and elbows scream at me, and I quickly tuck my arms down to my sides, where the pain is less. No one seems to notice, luckily.

"Okay, well, back to *our* moon," Pilot Gurkin says. "The Gateway station never traverses the far side of the Moon. Or it's sometimes called the dark side, because it's hidden from Earth, but it's not actually dark all the time. Real astronomers call it the far side. So, with its particular orbit always in view of Earth, Gateway has uninterrupted communications back home."

"Three more days 'til we're there, right?" David asks.

"'Are we there yet?' already?" Mae teases.

Pilot Gurkin chuckles. "Care to answer that one, Mae?"

"Sure. And yeah, about three days."

"Go on. What happens when we get there?" Pilot Gurkin prods.

"We'll intercept Gateway when it's farthest from the Moon," Mae continues. "We'll dock, after the Orion capsule moves out of its berth to accommodate the *Aether*, then drop off Specialist Barrera and Specialist Sokolov with the two crew there now. Gateway can support four people for thirty to sixty days before it needs refueling. Since the Gateway is only about a quarter the size of the ISS, it'd be too cramped if we all went in, so we'll take turns getting a short tour of the station, including the Habitation and Logistics Outpost. Or, the much cooler name: the HALO, where the US crew members live, plus the brand-new I-HAB, where the international crew bunks. We'll stay on the *Aether*, of course, during the couple days we're there. As we swing around closer to the Moon, you"—Mae points to Pilot Gurkin—"will fire the *Aether* away from Gateway. We'll check out the far side of the Moon, and use the Moon's gravity to help slingshot us back to Earth."

"You got all that?" Kal asks David.

"Can't wait," David says. "Sounds like fun, right?" He looks at me.

At that moment, I cringe. It feels like lightning behind my eyeballs. I might pass out. I want to say something, but my brain is suddenly not working properly.

"Fin, you don't look too good," David says.

"Oww" is all I can grunt.

"Wow, you're really pale. And you're sweaty." Kal puts her freezing cold fingers on my forehead. I flinch.

"He's burning up."

Pilot Gurkin feels my face too, then presses the button to speak over the comms to the astronauts on EVA. "Dr. Sokolov. We need you in here to take a look at Fin. Something's wrong."

My vision blurs, and I'm not sure what's happening. I feel more hands on me. Something wet on my forehead. I open my eyes, and I think it's Pilot Gurkin. With the sun shining in through the window behind her, in her white jumpsuit, she looks like an angel.

"I can't feel my legs," I mutter. My lips are hot.

Am I home? In the hospital? I remember the dream, waking up from the jet-ejection nightmare with sleep paralysis. But is it real now? Panic seizes me.

"I can't feel my legs," I repeat, louder. At least, I *think* I say it out loud. It sounds fuzzy.

I sort of blink out or doze off.

Sometime later, minutes or hours, I don't know, Dr. Sokolov is asking me questions. I say things, but I don't really know what. I can hear my words, but I don't feel in control of them. I keep nodding and saying, "Okay, okay," but I have no clue what she is asking or telling me to do.

Some part of me knows it isn't space sickness, because I'm not throwing up. But whatever is happening to me is not good. In the brief moments of lucidity, I'm scared.

Someone holds a water tube to my chapped lips, and I drink. For a brief moment, it helps.

Dr. Sokolov says something about "DCS," and David asks what that is, and Sokolov answers, but I can't understand. She unbuckles my harness. Now I'm moving.

Down the cabin, into the air lock.

This scares me even more. The air lock?

Wait.

What are they doing?!

Do I have some sort of space disease and they're jettisoning me out of the air lock before I can infect the others?

I realize I'm kicking and screaming only when Specialist Barrera pins me to the wall.

Pilot Gurkin and Dr. Sokolov are speaking in tones reserved for babies, trying to soothe me.

I fight Specialist Barrera with my sapped strength. Even in my optimal condition, I wouldn't be a match for the stocky man. But I get a good slug to his injured shoulder, and he groans. It doesn't last. He overpowers me and holds me down in the air lock.

I give in. I have to. I have nothing left. It hurts everywhere, and my brain is on fire.

Fine, just eject me out of here. Whatever. Just make the pain stop.

I close my eyes and cannot physically open them again. They are too heavy.

The weight of Barrera's body leaves me. I hear the air lock hatch shut and the depressurization buzzer.

It's only a matter of time now, and it'll be over.

When I come to, I feel squished over my whole body. Have I been restrained?

I open my eyes. I'm still in the air lock. They haven't vented me into space.

The thought that they would do that sounds ludicrous to me now. How could I have even imagined that? And the fact that I recognize that idea as ridiculous means I'm feeling more myself.

I touch all over my body. I wiggle my toes. I'm no longer paralyzed. I feel strangely better in this squished pressure.

David looks at me through the porthole window and then waves behind him for someone to come. A second later, Dr. Sokolov pushes the ATU intercom button, the audio terminal unit, so she can talk to me without opening the hatch.

"You were suffering from decompression sickness, Fin. DCS."

"It was a nasty case too, with late onset," Barrera adds. "The bends, like what scuba divers experience."

"We had to pressurize the air around you to help collapse the nitrogen bubbles in your body down to a normal level," Dr. Sokolov explains.

Just then my ears pop.

"Then we've been slowly bringing that pressure back to normal. Like a scuba diver ascending slowly."

"Am I going to be okay?" I rub my head.

Dr. Sokolov smiles. "Yes, you should be fine. No long-term damage. Though that headache might persist a while."

"How'd this happen? Didn't we depressurize for the space walks?"

"After talking it over, it sounds like, in your haste to rescue us, you didn't properly prepare for depressurization by breathing pure oxygen and exercising. Since the DCS symptoms can sometimes take hours, or even days, to show up, we didn't know there was a problem until after the event that triggered it. Your little body is not used to that kind of treatment!"

Little body? I don't point out we are about the same

size.

Besides being super thirsty, I feel way better than I did before I blacked out. I grimace, remembering that in my crazed state I thought they were going to fire me off into space! Oh, and I think I may have hurt Specialist Barrera's injured arm. Yikes.

"Hey, Barrera," I call out. His head appears in the window. "Sorry about that punch to your shoulder. Not cool."

He smiles. "I'm all right, Fin. Don't worry about it. But you should look into joining the wrestling team back at school. You're not bad."

Dr. Sokolov comes back on. "Shouldn't be too much longer in there, Fin."

"Thanks for the help," I say. And I realize that's the second time I've said something on this trip that I don't normally say.

Chapter 34

A few days later, after some *interesting* sleeps suspended in microgravity, with the Moon now looming larger in our window, Commander Horowitz reports that the damaged heat shield tiles have been replaced with new ones. There aren't enough spares left to do any further repair, so we have to be very careful about incurring any additional damage.

Pilot Gurkin adds that once we're docked at Gateway, we'll give the *Aether* a thorough inspection with the brand-new Canadarm3, a thirty-foot robotic arm. She crosses her fingers, and it seems like an awfully unscientific gesture. Nor does it instill confidence. Like we need a reminder that we might burn up in Earth's atmosphere?

As our ship approaches Gateway, I think back to when we first arrived at the ISS. Seems like forever ago. That glimmer of a star that got bigger and brighter and took on the shape of a weird metallic bug. The

Gateway is a fraction of the size of the International Space Station and more like a short, segmented caterpillar when compared with the sprawl of the ISS. Gateway is like its infant offspring, still in its cocoon stage. Well, with solar arrays spread out like butterfly wings. It's obviously a lot newer and, dare I say, *sparklier?* I bet it still has that new-station smell.

I remember pulling into the ISS, opening the hatch, and being greeted by our tour guide, Science Officer Christa Allaire.

I hold my hand in front of my face. It's shaking a little, again, like on the launchpad. I know in my head it's unlikely that the Gateway will suffer the same fate as the ISS, but I must admit it's not a zero chance.

There will be no one to greet us on the Gateway. The other two crew members here, Dr. Adam Lanni and Dr. Isaac DenOuden, are down on the Moon right now with the HLS, the Human Landing System.

As we're nearing the outpost, I see that the Orion capsule has already undocked from the end opposite the solar arrays and the Power and Propulsion Element. It's now attached to a docking port on the HALO. The Gateway doesn't have the distinctive elongated air lock module attached yet. I think that's being delivered next year by another of the Artemis missions.

"No," Kal corrects me after I say as much. "Next

year they get the ESPRIT, built by the European Space Agency and Japan. That's the European service module that handles refueling and communications."

"Uh, and the air lock?" I ask.

"Oh, right." She chuckles. "That's in two years."

"We're going to live up here without a means of doing EVAs until then," Specialist Barrera says, sounding wistful. "Unless we have the *Aether* docked and can use its air lock."

Hard to imagine he'd be so eager to get back out on a space walk after almost dying from one. These astronauts are human, sure, but a different breed than the average person.

"But," Dr. Sokolov adds, "we have the robotic arm from the Canadian Space Agency to do all our work for us. It is an amazing piece of engineering. It can move itself around our ship and reach everywhere. It can grab hold of supply shipments and secure them to a port. It's highly versatile."

After we dock via the automated system, we take turns checking out the Gateway. It's not entirely bigger than the *Aether*. In some ways, it feels like a step backward from the ISS just because it's smaller and still under construction. But in other, more important ways, it feels like the next giant leap forward. The tech, for one, is much more modern than on the ISS. It's cleaner, with less clutter on every surface.

"The Gateway is a staging ground," Dr. Sokolov says, "so that we, the US and all the international partners, can sustain a presence near and on the lunar surface."

"And it's great practice for going even farther into deep space." Barrera winks.

"Mars," David says. "Can't wait for that trip."

"Soon," Commander Horowitz agrees. "I might be getting too old for the first crewed Mars trip, but you're not. I think each and every one of you has demonstrated that you have what it takes, the right stuff, to be on those missions."

"Of course we do," Mae says.

"NASA has left low-Earth-orbit stations to the other countries and to the private companies building their own. We'll just rent space from private industry to maintain a US presence in LEO," Dr. Sokolov continues. "The Moon is the proving ground to go even farther. We've found literally tons of ice in the poles here. If we can harvest that ice—not only for water, but if we can break it down into oxygen to breathe and hydrogen for propellant—that would be a huge boost to our deep-space mission capability."

"The ISS is the past," I say. "Gateway is the future."

"Mars is the future," Kal says.

"The Gateway outpost is a stepping stone. Like the Gateway Arch in Saint Louis was to the western frontier," Specialist Barrera adds.

"On that note," Pilot Gurkin says with a smile, "we've inspected the *Aether* with Canadarm3, and Houston said—"

"Said we're clear," David butts in, "but we have to leave one person behind. Sorry, Fin."

"Hilarious," I say, rolling my eyes.

Pilot Gurkin gives David a polite chuckle. "Anyway, yes, the heat tiles passed inspection. So, Houston has cleared us for the trip around the Moon and determined that we are safe for reentry back to Earth."

"We're going home?" I ask.

"We're going home," she says.

Chapter 35

We say our goodbyes to Mission Specialist Glenn Barrera and Dr. Sally Sokolov. They both shoot out their arms for a handshake, but I reach and hug them both.

Specialist Barrera tousles my hair. I think about it revealing my birthmark, but do nothing to hide my crescent moon.

"Remember to check out the wrestling team when you get home." He chuckles.

"You both saved my life," I say. "I don't know how to say thank you for something like that."

Dr. Sokolov wipes a happy tear with her shirt. "It was you who saved us, Fin. What you did, crossing over to the ISS from the *Aether*?" She shakes her head in disbelief. "You didn't leave us behind. And Mae, Kalpana, David. If you hadn't been so stubborn"—she laughs, wiping another tear—"we would have gone down with the ISS. You are amazing, brave children, and your parents should be proud. Heck, the world should be proud."

I let go of the hug and float back to be next to my friends. The four of us make quite a team, and you can feel the earned pride we share in being recognized for our accomplishments. We see it in the way the mission specialists take one last look at us, for now.

"Well," Barrera says, nodding curtly. Is he choking back a tear too? "We better get to work. Lots to do around here. But feel free to visit anytime. Our door is always open. Well, not literally, 'cause then we'd get sucked into the vacuum of space, but you know what I mean."

I give him a chuckle.

Then we wave and close the hatch, sealing Dr. Sokolov and Specialist Barrera in the Gateway, alone.

Kal, David, Mae, Commander Horowitz, Pilot Gurkin, and I strap ourselves back into our jump seats on the *Aether*. It's time to slingshot around the Moon, going across the far side and back out into Earth's view.

Six of us left. Half of what we started with. We began this journey with twelve in the *Aether*, and it's now down to us. I glance at Uncle Dennis's empty seat. What would he think about seeing Gateway, about seeing the Moon so close you could see the shadows cast by the sun?

And Mr. Agarwal, Kal's dad. I know Kal misses him, and yet she's really shone with him not around to tell her what to do.

And Peggy, Mae's stepmom. I imagine how flummoxed she would have been to see Mae pilot a starship. That would have been priceless to witness. It would have put Peggy in a tizzy, for sure (one of her favorite words, not mine). It makes me laugh. Mae really is incredible, despite her hard exterior.

And Chris, David's dad. That round man reminded me of Tweedledee when I first met him, but then later, during the ISS crisis, when we heard his voice over the comms telling David to do what Houston told us, to save ourselves, he said it with such selfless conviction and bravery that he could have been ten feet tall.

But they aren't here now. It's just us. About to careen around the Moon, practically skimming the surface, closer than any kids have ever been.

The first kids in space. Our journey will go down in the history books.

Kids in school decades from now will learn my name.

Finley Scott, kid astronaut. Funny to think about that, but it does have a nice ring to it.

I wonder if this trip around the Moon will get as much time in that story as our struggle with the dying ISS. That was an exciting, dangerous, and near-fatal adventure, to be sure, and it deserves to be known. But getting so close to the Moon feels like more of an accomplishment.

We're about 240,000 miles away from our little blue planet.

Waaaaay out here, Earth is so small.

And I'm here with *these* five other people. I mean, it's cheesy, but . . . we're special, aren't we? I'm getting myself choked up.

I just hope *this* moment is remembered by all six of us more so than the one giant leap. Because despite that danger and death and trauma, *this* is what space travel is all about. Persistence. The pursuit of the great beyond. The push to keep going, *despite* the danger, or maybe because of it. There are risks, sure, but it's in our human nature to always strive to know what's around the next corner, what's on the next planet, and to learn more about our universe, maybe even our origins.

Hopefully, our trip is carving a path to Mars and opening up opportunities for other kids to visit the Moon too. And maybe someday, even interstellar travel.

I think about the opinions of people like Mr. Deuce, who aren't willing to take risks. And thus, no reward, no advancement.

Boy, did we prove him wrong.

The engines burn as we pull away from Gateway

and let the Moon's gravity take hold.

We're quiet, watching the gray rock below us fill the whole window.

We skim so close to the lunar surface, I want to reach out and grab a handful of that regolith, the shards of rock dust from countless asteroid impacts. We fly right over the landing area of Apollo 12, the site on the Moon where Conrad, Gordon, and Bean set an American flag, which didn't get knocked over like it did when Apollo 11 took off. Those Apollo 11 boys had planted the flag too close to the lunar module. When they burst off their perch to depart, the blast blew the flag over. That flag is buried in moondust now.

Through my binoculars, I see the Apollo 12 flag is bleached white from solar radiation, but it's still momentous. I've seen the Statue of Liberty, the Grand Canyon, the amber waves of grain . . . but seriously, nothing compares to seeing the flag on the Moon, near an old abandoned Moon rover. It is both majestic and kinda spooky.

I put my hand on my heart and start singing. "Oh, say can you see? By the dawn's early light—" My voice cracks, and I clear my throat to cover it up.

David looks at me blankly. I guess I don't know the Norwegian national anthem either.

Commander Horowitz smiles, genuinely, and salutes the flag.

Farther on, we see the HLS, and I point out a plume of dust from the two Gateway crew members—Adam Lanni and Isaac DenOuden—that we didn't get to meet. They're mining. But not for gold.

"There's the Chinese Yutu-2 rover," Pilot Gurkin points out. I see a tiny speck on the edge of a black chasm. "It's actually a reconnaissance lander for the Moon base they're planning to build."

The Surveyor crater beyond looms dark and menacing, and I can't help but be curious about what lies down in there. I think we all are. Mae peers over the edge of the window like she's trying to glimpse into the darkness.

Might be nothing but more rocks and dust. But is there ice down there? I wish good luck to the Gateway crew that they strike frozen "gold."

My thoughts are flying faster than we are whizzing over the surface. I want to slow us down and relish this experience. I want to go down there.

"Next time," Horowitz says.

"Next time," Mae adds, under her breath.

It wasn't long ago that I was adrift in space and thought I was going to die. I think about how the first people up here to the Moon must have felt. I wonder if they ever felt that sort of fear, that they were going to die. They must have, right? We've all heard the famous "Houston, we've had a problem" line. But they persevered through it. Humans made it to this Moon over half a century ago, and with so little technology compared with what we have now.

They were pioneers.

Like me.

I'm reflecting on all we've accomplished and still—still it seems like something is missing. I can't quite put my finger on it. Then the quote from Uncle D flashes into my mind again.

The hardest part is being honest with yourself. And once you figure that out, the next-hardest part is telling someone you can trust.

As we slip into darkness, I realize what that quote means for me, about being honest with myself, *and* with a trusted friend. It's clear what I need to do. What I *have* to do before I'll be ready to go back to Earth.

Chapter 36

While Commander Horowitz and Pilot Gurkin are watching the controls, the four of us kids keep our gaze out the window.

"I wish my parents were here to see this," I mutter. I am aware that my friends are floating next to me, but I don't look at them. If they don't take the bait and get me to keep talking, I might just let it slide.

We'd been observing speechlessly until I broke the silence, and when no one responds immediately, it's about what I should have expected. The internal lights are dimmed, and it's pretty much pitch-black outside, though we can sense the lunar surface gliding by below.

A few moments pass in the dark.

"Wish my dad were here to see this too," Kal says softly. "To see me."

"Yeah, my moms too," Mae adds, chewing on a fingernail.

I keep looking out the window. Part of me wants to let it go, but it's nagging me to let it out. I offer up the lure again. "My mom would love it up here."

I can tell David is nodding, but no one prods for any more.

Fine! I guess I'll just say it. I turn to them. "Hey, can I tell you guys something?"

"Course." David shrugs.

In the half-light, I can see Kal furrow her brow in curiosity and lean her head to the side. Mae nods.

Okay, here goes.

"When my mom—" I can't say it. This was a mistake. I'm embarrassed.

"Yes?" Mae asks, like it's no big deal.

But she doesn't know. It *is* a big deal. But just saying it shouldn't be, right?

"I was very scared when my mom's plane crashed." There. I said it. For the first time.

"I'm sure," Kal says. "When I read about how she ejected out of a fighter plane at Mach 1, I couldn't believe she survived. It's amazing, but it must have been terrifying for you."

David puts his hand on my shoulder. "Totally."

"Yeah, duh," Mae agrees. "That would be totally freaky. But your mom is pretty awesome. I want to be like her. I mean, a jet fighter pilot. Not the, uh, paralyzed part." Mae squirms.

Acknowledging that I'd been scared, out loud, and their accepting reactions kind of disarms the hold it has had over me all these months. Telling someone is easier than I thought it would be.

"It *was* terrifying," I add, repeating Kal's word for it, because it's perfect. "Going to the hospital. Wondering if she was going to die. I've been having nightmares about it. She's home now, but it's *still* scary. She's paralyzed; she's not herself. I mean, it scares me every time I see her. I'm scared about how to act around her, what to say, what not to say. And I've—I've never told anyone that before. Cheesy, I know. But, I don't know; I just had to tell you guys."

"At least she's around, right?" David says. "My mom's in prison with no chance of getting out for another ten years. Makes me angry."

I suddenly feel very selfish. "I'm sorry."

"Forget it," David says. He turns back to the window. "At least your mom is home."

It's blunt, but David is right. I think about Christa. Did she have kids?

I'd been trying to avoid the truth about my mom and run away from it, even escaping off-planet. But David is right. My mom is still alive, and I still have a life to live with her.

"You should bring her with us next time," Mae says. "In microgravity, you don't really use your legs that much." She pushes off from the wall with her hands and does a flip.

I notice that Kal is staring out the window at the sliver of horizon. Her chin quivers.

"With all the contracts NASA is going to give you for that SAFER escape system," Mae adds, still twirling, "I bet you'll be able to afford your own rocket ship to come up anytime you want."

I chuckle. "Next time, yeah."

I exhale a heavy sigh of relief like I'm not sure I've done in months. "Anyway, thanks for listening, guys."

David puts out his fist for a bump.

Instead, I give the three shakes for asteroid-moon-planet. He laughs and joins. He throws the crescent for moon. I hold my fist for planet.

"Dang it," he says, and shakes his head.

We turn to watch out the window again. I flash back to how good it felt to scream in space, where no one could hear me, by myself. Really, you should try it. Go in a closet or something, and just let it all out into a pillow.

But I realize that was only the first step, admitting my fear and frustration and anger to myself. I hadn't fully acknowledged that fear to a trusted friend. By being honest with myself, and then with someone else who was kind in return, I do feel a lot lighter now. I mean, I know I still have some heavy stuff to work through, but just saying it out loud sort of took away its power. At least, it made it smaller or more manageable, or like I wasn't alone. I don't know. It made it feel like something I can tackle. With help.

I think about the words from Uncle D again. He saw right through me this whole time. Maybe the funcle has some feelings after all.

Though I've been in microgravity for days now, I feel truly weightless for the first time.

"There's something I need to tell you guys too," Kal says. She pauses, looks around, then down. Opens her mouth, then closes it.

"Out with it," Mae says, impatient.

"I didn't want to go to space," Kal blurts, then grimaces.

My mouth opens in disbelief.

"What do you mean?" David asks.

"I'm claustrophobic, and I didn't want to go to space, and I didn't want to enter the StellarKid Project contest."

"Then why did you?" I ask.

"My dad," she says, looking at her fingers, picking at her nails. "He wanted me to enter, to win, so I did it for him. But I'm tired of doing things for him. And"—she looks up at us, pleading—"I'm really glad I came. Even with everything that happened. I wouldn't have you three as friends. So, maybe I owe my dad an apology."

"Well, sounds like he owes you an apology," Mae says.

"There's more," Kal says. She looks at me hesitantly.

"Okay." I nod, encouraging her to go on.

"I was approached by someone at JSC who asked me to sabotage the trainings. He knew I didn't want to go to space; he knew I am claustrophobic. He told me that I could get out of going to space if I just made us fail in the tests. He said no one would get hurt."

Wow. This is a bombshell.

"You sabotaged the centrifuge?" David asks.

"And the simulator?" Mae puts her hands on her hips and glares at Kal.

"Kal?" I look into her eyes. I can't believe she'd do something like this. It is such a betrayal.

"But I didn't do it!" She shakes her hands. Her purple strand of hair floats free, and she tucks it behind her ear. I can immediately tell she's being truthful.

Phew. If we were in a quiet room back home with gravity, you could hear a pin drop.

"But you didn't do it," David repeats, staring at her. It's half a question.

Kal matches the eye-lock. "No, I didn't."

"Why didn't you tell someone?" I ask.

"Because he said if I told, he'd frame me. I tried to find evidence, but he covered his tracks. It was his word against mine and—"

She didn't need to continue. As kids, we knew that it was most often the adult who won that showdown.

"I had to tell you guys. I had to come clean," she says. "Please forgive me." She looks each of us in the eye. "I'm—I'm scared."

I know that look. I just got done telling these friends I was scared too. I guess I inspired some brutal honesty in Kal, but boy, what a secret to be holding!

"Who was it?" I ask, but I think we all know the answer.

"Deuce," Mae sneers.

"Yes, it was Mr. Deuce," Kal says. "He's not an accountant."

"I knew there was something off about that guy," I say.

"Can you prove it?" David asks.

"Not at first, I couldn't. That's why I didn't say anything. I thought he was going to frame me. My dad would kill me," Kal says. "But when our comms were down, I had this terrible suspicion that it was him. So, I hunted around in the code. And I found irrefutable evidence of his tampering. He tried to hide it, but I found him out."

"Deuce was responsible for our comms blackout? Not the solar flare?" I ask. I had been out on my own with no radio, and it was Deuce's fault?

"As soon as I found the malware, I reversed it. That's how we got the comms back," Kal says.

"You definitely have to share this with the commander," I say. "That's attempted murder. He could have killed us."

"I know. I know. But I'm scared to," she says. "What will Deuce do if he finds out?"

"We'll be there with you," Mae says. "Deuce *has to* pay for what he did."

"Definitely," David adds, pounding his fist into his palm.

"Okay. I'll do it when we're back in comms range. And I will tell my father when we get home too," Kal says. She sighs. The way her shoulders relax, I think she feels better.

We're quiet again.

Mae fidgets and rolls her eyes. "Fine, I'll go."

"Oh, so is this a roundtable thing now? Honesty seems to be catching here." I grin.

"Look. I'm sorry if I can be a little, uh, grumpy," she says. Unlike Kal, Mae doesn't avert her eyes, almost daring us to agree. Or disagree. Or any reason to bark at us.

I don't take the bait and say nothing.

"It's just that, well, I have two moms. Which is, in itself, not a problem. But I live in South Africa. And one is Black, and one is white. And I'm mixed; my dad is white. So, you know, it's complicated. Not exactly your *typical* situation. And I'm sick and tired of people's dumb questions, and judgments, and—I don't know. I guess it can just make me snippy. Like I'm on guard more than maybe I should be all the time."

I nod my head ever so slightly.

She gives me the tiny little glimmer of a grin. "But you guys haven't treated me that way. You've been great. And I still kind of maybe made it hard for you, I guess. So, for that, I'm sorry."

"Thanks, Mae," I say. "For what it's worth, you are the best fourteen-year-old pilot I know."

"She's the only fourteen-year-old pilot you know," Kal chides.

"And still the best!" I put up a finger like she's number one. "Seriously, the way you handled the *Aether* was—it was not bad." I chuckle.

"Yeah, I'm pretty great," she says, but I can tell it's with a hint of teasing herself.

"You guys, I have a secret too," David breaks in. The way he says it with his palms out make it seem like it's going to be a heavy one. I can't imagine what the next revelation could be. Didn't he already share about his mom? What could be next? David is actually an alien sent to wipe out humans?

"I really have to poop," he says with a completely straight face. "That suction toilet scares me."

Mae rolls her eyes and sticks her tongue out in disgust. Kal looks relieved it's nothing dramatic. I groan and laugh and slug him in the shoulder.

"I just wish it scared the poop out of me," he says.

A bright slice of sunlight pierces into our cabin.

Commander Horowitz and Pilot Gurkin come floating over to join us.

"Here it comes!" Mae shouts. "Earthrise!"

The commander points his big fancy camera out the window.

We're glued to the glass.

There it is. Just a sliver of aquamarine cresting over the horizon of the Moon. Our little blue marble Earth, hanging in the galaxy all by itself. I get a deep longing, a sort of ache I haven't felt in months.

We're whipped out of the darkness and into the sunlight. I am filled by the beauty of the moment.

"Time to go home," Pilot Gurkin half whispers.

I nod. I'm ready.

Chapter 37

It takes three days to travel back to Earth, and I'm pretty sure David uses the suction toilet for number two only once in that whole time. Man, he must be stopped up.

I try to joke about this, but it comes out all wrong. Then I make a joke about it coming out all wrong, but the delivery gets messy and—

"Just stop," Kal says, putting her palm up to silence me.

We're strapped into our seats, getting ready for reentry. My jokes are no doubt because I'm trying to ignore my nerves. I hold my hand up.

Shaking. Slightly. But that's okay.

Will the heat shield hold? Commander Horowitz and Specialist Sokolov did their best to repair or replace the broken tiles, I'm sure, but plummeting through the atmosphere will heat our ship up to an incendiary 3,000 degrees Fahrenheit.

That is steel-melting hot.

I think of those seven *Columbia* astronauts, who spent their mission in space unaware that it would end in a fireball upon reentry. Like me, they thought they were on their way home to gravity and their own bed, a hot shower, and a toilet on which you can sit.

"*Aether*, this is Houston. We have a yellow conjunction. Sending the OCM data now."

You've got to be kidding me. Another space-junk warning?!

"Don't worry," Commander Horowitz tells us. "Happens all the time."

I can practically hear his wink.

The *Aether* starts to shimmy and vibrate as it drags in Earth's upper atmosphere.

"Houston, *Aether*. We're starting to feel the tug of Mother Earth here, which means we're going to lose comms for seven minutes," Pilot Gurkin says. While the ship reenters, the heat turns the air to plasma, which interrupts the radio signal. This is usually the longest seven minutes of the flight for ground control, since they have no way of knowing if we're safe or not. It also means we don't have much time to receive information on this potential conjunction.

"Shall we abort reentry?" Pilot Gurkin asks. I can tell she really doesn't want to hear an affirmative on that.

The *Aether* bounces, and Kal yips. It seems like a

minute passes, but I think it's only a few seconds.

"Houston, *Aether*," Pilot Gurkin says again. "We need a response *now*. Window for abort near terminus." I think that means it's now or never.

"*Aether*, Houston. Commence reentry." It crackles, but it's clear enough.

"And the OCM?" Horowitz asks.

"Green, Marc. Clear skies. Talk to you in—" The radio cuts out. We're on our own.

The extra gravity pushes me into the back of my seat.

Two g's, three g's, four. I can barely lift my arm.

"I'm freaking out!" Kal shouts, the static in our comms crackling loud.

"That makes sense!" I yell into my helmet.

"Woo-hoo!" Mae shouts.

"It'll be fine," David says, a little too forced. I think he's convincing himself.

Then he pukes into his helmet, chunks splattering on the glass. Gross.

I'm sorry, David, but I have to laugh. It's just such perfect timing.

It must be the return to gravity. The space sickness getting him again. Kal doesn't seem to be getting sick this time though, fortunately for her.

We plunge through the thickening air, getting buffeted around. It's hot. I hear explosions and metal creaking and groaning. Orange and yellow sparks, like we're inside a welder's torch, are streaming past the window, and I'm vibrating so hard in my seat I feel like my brain is going to pop out of my ears. This is much more intense than the forces of liftoff.

I close my eyes and grip my armrests. Nothing to do but hold on for the ride.

Then everything goes silent, and I float in my seat a little. Almost zero g.

Are we back in space? Did we miscalculate our trajectory and ricochet off of Earth's atmosphere like a stone across a flat lake? That means we're heading back into space and—

I'm jerked into my seat and hurled back so hard it feels like we're accelerating. That's not right either.

"Don't worry," Horowitz reports. "That's the main engine firing. The *Aether* made an automatic attitude adjustment."

I'm now staring up through a porthole at blue sky, and the thruster is rumbling heavily, and even though it feels like we're accelerating, I know the engine is slowing us down on our descent to the landing pad. A vertical landing. No ocean or capsule landing. We're touching down in the same position in which we blasted off, looking straight up.

Suddenly there's an extra blast, and we seem to hang in the air like a puppet for a split second. Then the string is cut, and there's a jolt, and the engine ceases. It shuts off immediately. I hear the hiss of some sort of exhaust.

"*Aether* touchdown nominal," comes over the comms. Loud. And. Clear.

Ah, what a relief!

That level of dry emotion from Houston is nowhere near as exuberant as I feel.

I shout a "woo-hoo!"

The others cheer too.

Even David pumps his fists in the air with slime running down the inside of his helmet. It's gross, and hilarious.

I am overflowing with feelings of relief and excitement and . . .

"Again!" I exclaim, the same refrain I'd scream as a little kid when my dad threw me into the air.

The steam and smoke clear, and I can see out the *Aether's* window, in the pale blue sky, a tiny sliver of the waxing crescent moon. That means it'll get brighter in the days ahead, until it's full. Kind of like how I feel right now.

I remember seeing the Moon as a thumbnail when we were sitting on the launchpad. I think of that kid as someone else, someone who'd never been to space or jumped across the void to save others.

And now, this same-but-different kid is waiting to

end one journey and begin another. I think about nearly drowning in space, then about Kal's software that saved me. I remember Christa's necklace bouncing away from her face as she blew on it softly. Dr. Sokolov and the decompression chamber that saved me from the bends. Gateway, and the shadows on the Moon, and the HLS upright on the surface. The bleached-white Apollo 12 flag still standing strong. Such amazing things I've seen. And friends I've made for life.

The *Aether* monitors turn into video feeds of a crowd, cheering, holding banners that say "Welcome back!" and "Earth missed you!" A marching band is playing, the golden bell of the swaying tuba catching the sunlight. The camera cuts to a close-up scene of the front rows, the VIP section. I see Uncle Dennis smiling and waving, with one arm around Shelley, our PR coordinator. Mr. Agarwal with a woman in a sari who I assume is Kal's mom. Next to them is Peggy, with another woman I assume is Mae's mom. Then, David's dad, alone. I think about David's mom, in prison.

They're all beaming and waving and clapping.

Then the camera pans to a woman in a wheelchair. I'd recognize that huge smile anywhere. My mom holds a cardboard sign that says, "We're proud of you!" Cheesy, Mom. Typical. Next to her, my dad waves two signs. One that says "We're all going" and the other "Next time."

I laugh, my fist to my mouth. "Next time."

"Sure. Next week, same time?" Mae asks.

"Sign me up. But first, I have some things I need to talk over with my mom and dad."

Being honest with them doesn't feel like it will be such a giant leap.

Epilogue

Kal's evidence served to incriminate Mr. Deuce, who was actually revealed to be a covert foreign agent. NASA security protocols were hardened to prevent another intrusion, but the threat is constant, and enemies of the space program, and of the US, require constant vigilance.

Science Officer Christa Allaire was awarded, posthumously, the Presidential Medal of Freedom. We were all there to share in the ceremony: me; my parents; Uncle Dennis and his new girlfriend, Shelley; the Agarwals; the Jorgensons; the Kalkuttens; Commander Horowitz and Pilot Gurkin; the ISS crew that served with Christa; and even Specialists Barrera and Sokolov via video call with a two-and-a-half-second delay from the Moon. As well as many others in person and thousands via streaming service.

The ISS's catastrophic loss will be analyzed for years to come, but preliminary analysis confirmed it was indeed space junk that did her in. Mae's StellarKid Project proposal for new craft requirements to minimize space junk was passed unanimously by Congress and the international spacefaring countries as an addendum to the Outer Space Treaty, all of which dubbed it the Mae Jorgenson Clean Space Act. Axis Space is investing in technologies to harvest existing space junk to take to the Moon as raw material.

David's V-Air video game system went on to sell millions of units after it was announced you could play with real astronauts in space. He called me one day to say that he'd visited his mom in prison and told her how he felt, and that she'd been so happy to see him. "Lighter than air" is how he described the feeling.

Kal's algorithms landed her a teaching gig at Caltech, promised to her after she graduated from college. She finally confronted her dad about forcing her into things she didn't want to do, but she also thanked him for pushing her to succeed, since she wouldn't have been to the Moon if it wasn't for him.

As for the SAFER, well, I'm honored to report that it will be employed as standard equipment during every space walk. The company we formed to supply the gear, SAFER Space, Inc., is doing very well.

And, though I haven't flown with Mae, David, and Kal again—yet—I do have another rocket launch booked, to fly to the Moon next spring. We'll put boots on the surface this time. And, I'm happy to say, I bought a seat for my mom and dad too.

Author's Note: Fact v. Fiction

This was an *immensely* fun book to research and to write. I happily went down countless rabbit holes and tried to make the details and history in the story as realistic as possible, while also taking some creative liberties to make it an action-packed novel. In this section, I'll talk about a few of the key items in this story, and where they lie on the spectrum of fact versus fiction.

First of all, the SAFER is real. If you knew that fact when you started reading this story, then good for you. I hope it didn't detract from the fantasy. Personally, I didn't know about it when I started this project. As Fin mentioned, inventing something new for space travel is perplexingly difficult because of the vast quantity of really smart people who have, for decades, been thinking about the challenges of living and working in space. I actually dreamed up a jet pack as a life preserver of sorts for astronauts, probably after watching the 2013 movie *Gravity*, which stars Sandra Bullock. In that movie, she becomes detached from the ISS after debris wipes out the station. I thought a mini jet pack could have saved her in that situation, though it probably would have made the rest of the movie far less dramatic. Only in researching later did I learn about the SAFER. In fact, that is one complaint real astronauts cite about the movie. I hope they will forgive me for a similar transgression. Also, the AAH is real. The video game remote was prototyped, but never deployed, using an Xbox controller. Anyway, I hadn't heard of the SAFER, nor had most of the general population, who, like me, loved the movie *Gravity*. So, I took the idea and gave it to Fin. It fit nicely with my original vision for Fin's emotional journey, and serves as a good teaching moment via this note!

While I was brainstorming the plot for this novel, I felt inspired by the idea of a rich person buying some seats for kids to go to the Moon. In researching the idea of civilians going to space, and to the Moon in particular, I learned about two very important, and very real, projects.

First, I learned about dearMoon (dearmoon.earth), in which a Japanese artist purchased eight seats on the SpaceX Starship, planned for a trip around the Moon in 2023. Maybe by the time you read this, that has already happened. Or, as can be expected with giant projects as complicated as this, maybe there will be delays.

Second, and more recent to this writing, the SpaceX Inspiration4 mission successfully launched the first all-civilian crew into space (inspiration4.com). They orbited the Earth higher than the ISS for three days before returning safely. Learning about their journey, and watching along with them, was truly an inspiration. And SpaceX also launched the Ax-1 all-civilian crew to the ISS in April of 2022.

I've cited SpaceX here because it is currently the dramatic leader in commercial space missions. Its reusable Falcon Heavy booster, along with the Dragon capsule, is regularly ferrying cargo and crew to the ISS. Boeing is also working on a solution, called Starliner. It has hit some scheduling issues and is behind, but they're not giving up, and by the time Fin goes on his journey, I imagine there will be others.

The ISS is, technically, past its operating lifetime. Assuming it is still up there when you read this, you can track its location here: spotthestation.nasa.gov.

As of this writing, Congress renewed its budget through 2030. Whether it will live past then is up for debate, but I personally find it hard to believe we'll just scrap it at that point. For many reasons, but one that is concrete: a company named Axiom has contracted with NASA to use the ISS as a staging area to assemble its commercial station and share resources like power and life support. That is, until it can live on its own, at which point it will break off from the ISS and be fully self-sustaining. This is one aspect of the "commercialization of space" that was mentioned in this book. NASA supports and partially subsidizes the development of private stations like Axiom, with the idea that it'll rent space from them down the road, similar to how it's using SpaceX as a taxi and cargo service. This will help to ensure the US maintains a presence in LEO.

In addition, Russia and China are starting their own space stations. Time will tell how far these evolve, but it will be very interesting to see what happens in LEO over the next ten years.

It's true that NASA is focusing on the Artemis missions, to take the first woman and the next man to the Moon in 2025. (Note: When I started this story, the plan was to get them there in 2024.) The Artemis program also includes construction of the Gateway outpost, orbiting the Moon. Gateway will enable earthlings to maintain a more permanent presence on and around the lunar surface. It will also serve as a staging ground for missions to Mars. While the Moon is an amazing goal in itself, pretty much everyone who talks about Artemis, and Gateway, can't help but also slip in the big dream of sending humans to Mars.

Many of the names in this book were used in tribute to important people in the history of space exploration. Of note, the characters I invented likely share no actual personality characteristics with their namesakes; I used their names simply as an excuse to bring them into this note. They are listed in alphabetical order below.

Chris Hadfield: Mentioned by name. A very real Canadian astronaut. He really did play "Space Oddity" on his guitar aboard the ISS. It is a very impactful video. He's also made many other videos, demonstrating things like how to brush your teeth and sleep in space. He's an accomplished astronaut and commander, and he seems like an all-around good guy with whom I wouldn't mind sharing a meal. If you're reading this, Chris, let's do it.

Christa: Christa McAuliffe, the American schoolteacher who died in the space shuttle *Challenger* tragedy in 1986.

David: David Mackay, the first Scot to visit space.

Dennis: Dennis Tito, an American, the first tourist to space in 2001.

Eileen: Eileen Collins, the first woman to pilot the space shuttle.

Glenn: John Glenn, the first American to orbit Earth.

Kalpana: Kalpana Chawla, the first woman of Indian descent in space. She died in the space shuttle *Columbia* tragedy in 2003.

Mae: Mae Jemison, the first African American woman in space.

Marc: Marc Garneau, the first Canadian in space.

Peggy: Peggy Whitson has more time in space than any other American. Between 2002 and 2017, Whitson had three long hauls on the International Space Station, where she spent 665 cumulative days in space. She was the first female astronaut to command the ISS twice. She spent over sixty hours in EVA. And a bunch of other stuff. You should read about her. She also works with Axiom Space now, so no doubt she'll be returning off-planet.

Rakesh: Rakesh Sharma, the first Indian citizen in space.

Sally: Sally Ride, first American woman in space. She set the record for the youngest American in space at age thirty-two in 1983 until her record was broken by Hayley Arceneaux at age twenty-nine aboard the SpaceX Inspiration4 in 2021.

Scott: Scott Kelly, an American astronaut who spent 340 days on the ISS along with a Russian counterpart to study the long-term effects of microgravity on the human body. His twin, astronaut Mark Kelly, was studied in tandem while on Earth for comparison.

Toyohiro: Toyohiro Akiyama, the first person of Japanese descent in space, whose trip was commercially funded by the Japanese TBS TV to celebrate its fortieth year and to gain viewers. He was a reporter at the time.

Valentina: Valentina Tereshkova, from Russia, holds a number of records. She was the first female astronaut, the youngest, and the only woman to have been on a solo space mission. She was twenty-six when she orbited the Earth forty-eight times over three days in 1963.

And I'm not done with this section yet! Like I said, researching for this book was so fun, and I want to share that joy with you.

I would be remiss if I didn't mention that the incident with the water in the space suit is based on a real crisis experienced by Italian spacewalker Luca Parmitano in 2013. I'll let you learn more about that on your own. I watched a video of Luca when he got back into the ISS, and he is remarkably more calm than I would be (or than Fin was) if I had water in my helmet!

It's also true that an astronaut plugged a hole he found on the ISS with his thumb. Temporarily, at least. In 2018, the ISS crew woke up to an alarm of air escaping the ISS, and when ESA astronaut Alexander Gerst found the two-millimeter hole in the orbital compartment of the Soyuz, he stopped the leak with his thumb. Later, they used glue and Kapton tape to seal it while devising a more permanent solution.

There are probably many more tweaks I gave to reality, such as the fact that the centrifuge is actually at Ames Research Center in California, not at JSC.

On that note, a broader comment on accuracy: Though I have tried to ring true to the general procedures used on the ISS, and in launches, and in space travel, I have obviously grossly oversimplified things for the sake of the action. For example, the Shuttle documentation for EVA procedures is hundreds of pages and would quickly bore my readers!

I'm sure there are thousands of other factoids I could share with you, but that would quickly bloat this book into a nonfiction one tacked on to the end of a fiction story, so I'm going to force myself to end here. Hopefully, I've piqued some categories of interest, which will give us more we can talk about when we see each other next.

My final, closing note is this: One of the dangers of writing a "realistic" space fiction novel is how all of this may change by the time you read it. I risk the danger of being out-of-date even before publication day. Or I may get some of it wrong. But, at the same time, I believe there's a timelessness to this particular moment in the epic of space travel that, hopefully, I have helped to capture with this little story.

The details may change, but the spirit will remain.

Glossary

Aether (pronounced EE-ther): The fictional starship taken into space by the StellarKid Project winners. Named after the "upper sky" in Greek mythology which only the gods could breathe.

ARED: The Advanced Resistive Exercise Device, which provides muscle stimulation via resistance exercises aboard the International Space Station.

Artemis: A NASA program whose missions will return humans to the Moon.

centrifuge: A machine that rotates rapidly to simulate extra g-forces.

Challenger: The space shuttle that exploded seventy-three seconds into its flight on January 28, 1986.

CME: A coronal mass ejection, a large sun-burp (he-he) of plasma and magnetic field from the sun's corona, which may cause disturbances in radio transmissions and electronics in LEO and on Earth.

Columbia: The space shuttle that exploded upon reentry on February 1, 2003.

cupola: The windowed area on the ISS with 360-degree views toward Earth.

DCS: Decompression sickness, commonly called

the bends, occurs when nitrogen in the blood forms bubbles as pressure decreases. May cause a range of symptoms, including nausea and aches, and even result in death.

debris avoidance maneuver: An ISS procedure to avoid collision with space debris. Relatively routine every year.

delta-vee: A change in velocity.

Destiny module: The primary US research lab on the ISS.

EMU: An extravehicular mobility unit, more commonly known as a space suit, which enables astronauts to work in the vacuum of space.

ESPRIT: The European System Providing Refueling, Infrastructure and Telecommunications, a Gateway outpost module.

EVA: An extravehicular activity, more commonly known as a space walk.

Gateway: The Gateway outpost, a station that will orbit the Moon as part of the Artemis program.

G-LOC: A g-force-induced loss of consciousness.

HALO: The Habitation and Logistics Outpost, a Gateway module that will expand the number of people that can stay aboard the vessel.

Harmony module: Known as the utility hub of the ISS, connecting the modules of the US, Europe, and Japan and providing power and data capabilities.

HLS: The Human Landing System, which astronauts will use to get from Gateway down to the Moon.

ISS: The International Space Station, a football-field-size research facility that has been orbiting Earth since its construction began in 1998.

IVA: An intravehicular activity, similar to an EVA, a space walk, but within the confines of a depressurized vehicle.

Joint Space Operations Center (JSpOC): The center that tracks, catalogs, and monitors artificial objects orbiting Earth, including all inactive and active satellites, spent rocket bodies, and fragmentation debris (aka space junk!).

JSC: Johnson Space Center, NASA's human spaceflight hub since 1965.

Kármán line: The boundary between Earth's atmosphere and outer space, 100 kilometers (62 miles) above Earth.

LEO: Low Earth orbit, where the ISS resides, approximately 250 miles above Earth.

MECO: Main engine cutoff, the point during a staged rocket launch at which the main engine quits, before it separates and the second stage fires.

MMOD: Micrometeoroids and orbital debris, also known as space junk.

NASA: The National Aeronautics and Space

Administration, the US government body responsible for the space program.

NOAA: The National Oceanic and Atmospheric Administration, whose Space Weather Prediction Center monitors the sun for coronal mass ejections.

NRHO: A near-rectilinear halo orbit, a squished oval that comes very close to the body it orbits on one of its passes. The Gateway outpost will be on an NRHO around the Moon.

OCM: An Orbital Conjunction Message, a warning from mission control that a piece of space debris is forecast to intersect with a spacecraft's trajectory. There are various degrees of severity, and an OCM may warrant a debris avoidance maneuver.

Orion capsule: A capsule atop the Space Launch System that will take astronauts back to the Moon as part of the Artemis missions.

PMA-2: The pressurized mating adapter mounted on the forward port of the Harmony module where ships can dock when visiting the ISS.

Power and Propulsion Element (PPE): One of the most important modules of Gateway.

Quest air lock: The air lock on the US side of the ISS where astronauts can depressurize and voyage out into the vacuum of space in their EMUs.

SAFER: The Simplified Aid for EVA Rescue, a jet-pack-like attachment astronauts wear on their backpack life-support system that can safely return them to the ISS if they become detached. It operates with spurts of gaseous-nitrogen from twenty-four thrusters. In this story, it is fictionally the invention of Finley Scott, one of the winners of the StellarKid Project.

Saturn V: The rocket that took the Apollo missions to the Moon in the late 1960s and early 1970s.

SLS: The Space Launch System, a massive rocket system that will take the Orion capsule to the Moon as part of the Artemis missions.

Soyuz: A Russian workhorse rocket that has flown since the 1960s, launching thousands of flights ferrying crew and cargo into space.

Space Surveillance Network: A combination of optical and radar sensors used to support the Joint Space Operations Center.

TCA: The time of closest approach, relayed in an OCM when a piece of space debris is forecast to cross orbits with the ISS or other spacecraft.

trans-lunar injection (TLI): The powerful rocket firing that sends a vehicle out of Earth's orbit and on its way to the Moon.

Tranquility module: The module on the ISS with exercise equipment, environmental-control systems, a toilet, and the cupola.

Unity module: The first US-built component of the

ISS, which connects the US and Russian segments.

Van Allen belts of radiation: Zones of energetic charged particles, originating from solar wind, held around a planet by its magnetosphere. Earth has two and sometimes more. Crossing through these can give astronauts a dose of radiation.

Yutu-2 rover: A Chinese rover that is the longest-lived lunar rover.

Zvezda module: The center of the Russian segment of the ISS, where crew members gather in case of emergency.

About the Author

Ben Gartner is the award-winning author of adventure books for middle graders. His stories take readers for a thrilling ride, maybe even teaching them something on the journey. Ben can be found living and writing near the mountains with his wife and two boys.

BenGartner.com
Twitter: @BGartnerWriting
Instagram: @BGartnerWriting

CPSIA information can be obtained
at www.ICGtesting.com
Printed in the USA
LVHW110731010223
738326LV00002B/28